CHOSEN PATH

EDGE OF THE WORLD SERIES : BOOK 1

LEROY A. PETERS

PRODUCTIONS

ISBN: 9798544716181

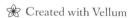 Created with Vellum

1

"Massa John, Massa John!" shouted Edward as he came running up to the main house from the field. John Allen and his eldest son, John Jr., quickly looked up from the paperwork that contained plans for their cotton business. Edward was running as if the devil himself was after him. The black slave came to a halt at the porch, almost out of breath, his eyes wide with shock and fear.

Surprised at the slave's expression, John Allen asked, "What's wrong, Edward?" John had no idea what could have put such a scare in Edward. The Allen plantation was known for its fairness, despite owning the one hundred slaves that worked his cotton fields. It was rumored that there were no mulatto babies born among his slaves, and a black woman, slave or free, was safe on the Allen farm. *So what has Edward so pale?* John wondered.

"Massa John, it's Miss Abigail, Reverend Hancock's little girl!" Edward was by this time almost to the point of crying.

John Allen's expression grew more serious. Fourteen-year-old Abigail Hancock was the only daughter of his best friend, Reverend Nehemiah Hancock.

"What about her?" he asked, his voice trembling with apprehension.

"She was found down by the creek, sir. Somebody beat her and... oh, God!"

Both John and John Jr. jumped to their feet at his words. "Where is she now?" asked John Jr.

"Your brothers, Massa James, Robert, and young Jason, are carrying her here right now. They sent me ahead to tell you."

Father and son sprang into action. John Sr. had Edward fetch Mabel. She was not only the house cook but an expert in medicine and healing. Although she was a free woman, she had stayed on after Massa John had signed the manumission papers for her, her husband, and son. *Whatever has happened to Abigail Hancock, Mabel would be able to fix and heal, at least physically*, thought John Sr. When Abigail was brought into the house and John Sr. saw her for the first time, he had to quickly control himself. The description that Edward gave of what was done to Abigail was an understatement. Someone had not only brutally beaten her but had raped her repeatedly. Her clothes were torn to shreds, she was almost naked, and barely conscious.

John Sr. wasn't the only one who was outraged. His youngest son, Jason, who was the same age as Abigail and madly in love with her, was even more so. Alice, John's wife, immediately ordered to have Abigail sent to the master bedroom. Mabel was not far behind and quickly got to tending her.

"Abigail," asked Alice. "Can you hear me, child?" Abigail was barely conscious, but she managed to respond to the woman she affectionately called Aunty Alice. She nodded. "Who did this to you, child?" asked Alice.

"Belshazzar Jones," answered Abigail with some struggle. "He, he attacked me on my way home from the store in town."

"DAMN!" shouted John Allen Sr.

"John, please, no cussing," said Alice.

"Woman, my best friend's only daughter is lying there beaten and raped by a man who not only despises her family, but his daddy

2

also is the county sheriff and his uncle is a judge, and you're worried about me saying a forbidden four-letter word!"

Less than a minute later, John calmed down and told his sons, Robert and Jason, to head over to the church and tell Abigail's parents and her brother that they needed to come immediately, but not to tell them what happened yet.

2

Reverend Nehemiah Hancock was just finishing up his papers that he had written for his upcoming sermon on Sunday. The forty-two-year-old Baptist preacher was not your typical hellfire and brimstone type with a lack of a sense of humor. He was also not the kind of man you would expect to be a preacher, after one look at him. At six-foot-eight and two hundred and eighty pounds of rock-solid muscle, Reverend Hancock was intimidating. Of English descent and a descendant of one of the Mayflower refugees, Nehemiah found his calling to preach the good news after serving in the War of 1812.

A staunch abolitionist and a follower of the early seventeenth century New England Puritan preacher Roger Williams, who was a staunch supporter of American Indian rights and an abolitionist himself, Reverend Hancock was a man ahead of his time as far as race relations, equality, and religious tolerance were concerned, more than his neighbors cared for or wanted. He strongly believed that all men and women, regardless of skin color or religion, were equal in the eyes of God, and he was not afraid to practice what he preached.

A secret conductor of the famous Underground Railroad, many runaway slaves owed their freedom to the good reverend and his family. His devoted wife of fifteen years, thirty-five-year-old Abigail, shared her husband's convictions. While most marriages of that time were based on necessity, the marriage of Nehemiah and Abigail was truly love at first sight.

Born in Harrisburg, Pennsylvania, the daughter of Scottish immigrants, Abigail MacDonald moved to Baltimore, Maryland, when she was nineteen, looking for a job as a teacher. It was there she met Nehemiah, a rock farmer's son, who was gentle as a lamb, but tall as Goliath. After a year of courtship, the twenty-seven-year-old future preacher and twenty-year-old school teacher were married on Valentine's Day in 1805. On January 1, 1806, Abigail gave birth to fraternal twins: a girl, which Nehemiah named after her mother and affectionately called Little Abigail. Then two minutes later, a son, whom Abigail named Azariah Daniel Hancock.

Reverend Hancock and his wife were different as night and day. To say that they were complete opposites was an understatement, according to those that knew them. While the good reverend was a giant block of muscle of a man, Abigail was short and pudgy at five-foot-two. While the reverend had a huge sense of humor and didn't take life too seriously as most preachers of his time did, his wife was always serious about everything and had a bit of a temper. What they did share was the love of their children, love for God, and love for people. Both parents were strict and staunch believers in 'spare the rod, spoil the child,' but they were also loving and taught Little Abigail and Azariah humility, standing up for what is right, picking and choosing your battles, and the benefits of hard work.

When he wasn't preaching, Reverend Hancock and his family were always busy on their farm, where they raised corn, goats, sheep, hay, and tobacco. Farming is what helped Reverend Hancock develop strong muscles on his large frame. His son, Azariah, was not that far behind. The youth inherited his father's strength and height. By the time he and his sister turned fourteen, three months previously, he already had grown to six-foot-six and weighed a muscular two hundred and sixty pounds. Little Abigail inherited her mother's height, being five-foot-five, but was slimmer and petite. The family was strong and close-knit, which they had to be. Being an abolitionist in slaveholding Montgomery County, Maryland was not a place where you could make friends. However, that changed after the War of 1812, before Nehemiah became a minister.

During the war, he befriended John Allen and saved his life at the Battle of Horseshoe Bend. When the two returned home after the war, they not only became neighbors, but life-long friends and allies, even though John and his family owned over a hundred slaves. Over the years, the Hancock children would play with the Allen children, and it was no secret that Jason Allen, John's youngest son, had a crush on Abigail. With her father's permission, the two would always go horseback riding, either in the woods or on the Allen plantation, and Jason would always have her back home before her curfew.

Azariah was always shy around girls and preferred to be by himself a lot. This mostly had much to do with his family being not well-liked in the community, even though he considered many of the Allen boys, as well as the slaves on the Allen plantation, good friends. When he wasn't helping on the farm, he would go off alone and hunt turkey and white-tailed deer and bring them home. His father taught him how to skin game when he was old enough to pick up a rifle, so this had become second nature to him. Azariah was doing exactly that on his recent kill when he saw Robert and Jason Allen riding up the road towards his house as if the devil himself was on their heels.

"Azariah, are your parents home?" asked Robert, who was older than both his brother and Azariah by six years.

"They're inside the house," answered Azariah. "What's wrong?"

Jason was about to answer, but his brother stopped him. Hearing the commotion, Reverend Hancock stepped outside and was about to greet the young men, but quickly sensed that something was wrong.

"Reverend," said Robert. "You, Mrs. Hancock, and Azariah better come with us."

"What is wrong, Robert?" asked the reverend.

Robert hesitated, but then decided to tell him. "It's Abigail, sir. Jason and some of our servants found her down by the creek."

Not even twenty minutes later, Reverend Nehemiah Hancock and his wife, Abigail, were at their daughter's side at the Allen plantation. John and Alice explained to them what she told them. Nehemiah could not contain his rage after seeing what Belshazzar Jones did to his daughter. Not even his wife had ever seen him that angry.

"Stay with Little Abigail," said the reverend.

Abigail did not like the sound of that. "Where do you think you're going?" she demanded.

"Just stay with our daughter. She will need you when she wakes up," he responded.

"No, Nehemiah, she needs both of us," said Abigail as she stood between her husband and the door.

John and Alice, who were listening, stood next to her to keep Nehemiah from doing something rash. However, it was Mabel who spoke.

"Rev'end Hancock, don't go do nuthin' foolish," she said. "Miss Abigail is right. Your daughter needs you, and you will be no good to her if you're dead."

"Mabel is right, Nehemiah," added John. "I know how you are feeling right now. You forget I have three daughters of my own, and Little Abigail is like my own daughter. Nothing would satisfy me more than to see Belshazzar Jones pay for what he did to her, but you have to remember, you are a man of God now. Vengeance goes against everything you believe in and everything you have taught."

Nehemiah's blood was boiling, but he knew John was right. Still, this was his daughter and he wanted revenge. He knew, like everyone else, that Belshazzar Jones was not going to be arrested or tried for raping the daughter of the town's nigger-loving preacher. But something had to be done.

"Daddy?" the small, struggling voice brought the good reverend back to his senses as he and his wife turned to see their daughter awake.

"I am here, Little Abby," he said as he approached her bedside. Tears welled up in both parents' eyes as they held their daughter's hand.

"I am sorry, Daddy," said Little Abigail.

"Sorry for what?"

"I tried, I tried to fight him off. He was too—"

"You hush now, child," said mother Abigail. "It is not your fault. It was him and him alone. And one way or another, he will pay for what he did to you."

"Your mother is right," said the reverend. "Right now, rest. We will not leave your side."

So entrenched was everyone in caring for Little Abigail that no one paid attention when Azariah left the room. No one noticed him leaving the Allen plantation except Jason Allen, who said nothing.

3

Later that evening, Belshazzar Jones was walking through the woods on his way home. His family's plantation was not as big as the Allens', but they owned at least twenty slaves, which was enough to run it, and additionally, his father was the town constable. The twenty-year-old had just bragged to his friends at Harper's Tavern how he poked Abigail Hancock, the daughter of the nigger-loving preacher. She was not the first woman he raped. In fact, for his fourteenth birthday, his father gave him a slave girl as a rite of passage to manhood. Since then, Belshazzar had had his way with three black women from his father's farm and two from his uncle's plantation.

Abigail Hancock was not the first white woman he ever raped, but the first victim to ever fight back. That turned him on. Black slave women, whom he called his harem, never fought back, mainly because they feared the consequences of what would happen if they did. The idea of a woman fighting back gave him an excitement that he never dreamed of. "I think I will poke the nigger-loving preacher's daughter again, first chance I get," he said to himself. Engrossed in his thoughts, he didn't notice someone standing in his path, holding a loaded blunderbuss and pointing it at him.

"That is far enough, you sick bastard," said Azariah.

Belshazzar Jones stared at the large youth, and realizing the gun was pointed at him, he laughed.

"Well, ain't that sweet. Come to defend the honor of that whore of a sister."

Azariah's blood began to boil. He was about to pull the trigger, but he had a feeling that he shouldn't.

"You ain't got the guts, preacher boy," taunted Belshazzar. "After all, what would your daddy say with all that talk of 'vengeance is mine, sayeth the Lord' nonsense?"

Azariah didn't lower the blunderbuss; he just stood there, still hesitant, while Belshazzar continued to laugh and taunt him.

"That's what I thought. As for your sister, I think I will visit her and give her another poke, maybe bring some friends to join in and you can watch!"

That did it. Azariah, without hesitation this time, raised the blunderbuss at Belshazzar Jones and fired. The blast and its force sent the rapist over four feet from where he stood. He landed on a tree with a hole in his chest the size of grapeshot. Azariah walked up to his sister's dying rapist. Belshazzar Jones was wheezing, gasping for air.

"I'll be damned, you son of a—" were Belshazzar's last words.

"You are indeed damned," said Azariah. "For what you did to my sister!"

4

The next morning, Nehemiah and Abigail were having breakfast at their daughter's bedside, while she was recuperating on the Allen plantation. It dawned on them the night before that their son was missing. John Allen Sr. and his two eldest sons, John Jr. and William, along with one of the slaves, Champ, went out searching for him.

"I hope Azariah hasn't gone and done anything foolish," said Abigail.

Nehemiah said nothing. He was torn between being a preacher and following the teachings from the Bible about vengeance, and being a father whose only daughter was brutally raped and his missing son probably had gone to take matters into his own hands.

As if reading her husband's thoughts, Abigail gently placed a hand on his. "It is in God's hands, Nehemiah," she said. "All we can do is pray that justice will prevail."

"I know, I know, Abigail." Nehemiah couldn't stop his hands from shaking as he gently squeezed his wife's hand. "For God's sake, she is our daughter. I should've never let her go into town by herself!"

Before anyone could say more, John entered the room with a dour look on his face.

"Did you find Azariah?" asked Nehemiah.

"Yes, we found him, and he is safe," answered John. "But we got a problem, Nehemiah, a big one."

"What happened?" asked Abigail.

"Belshazzar Jones was murdered last night. His body was found early this morning, not far from his daddy's plantation, with a hole in his chest the size of grapeshot."

Nehemiah and Abigail looked at each other as if they knew who was responsible before asking John, "Azariah?"

"He confessed to us when we found him by the creek a mile from here," answered John. "I have him hiding under my barn, and it won't be long before Sheriff Jones comes calling with a lynch mob."

"Oh, sweet Jesus!" shouted Abigail. Nehemiah and John calmed her down when Little Abigail woke up.

"Daddy, what's happening?" she asked.

Seeing no reason to lie to her, Nehemiah gently sat next to her bed and calmly told her what her brother did. Tears welled in her eyes, mainly because she was concerned about what would happen to her brother.

As expected, Sheriff Frederick Jones and his so-called deputies showed up on the Allen plantation. He, like everyone in Montgomery County, knew that the Allen and Hancock families were close friends, and when he could not find Azariah Hancock at his home or his daddy's church, the Allen plantation was the next stop.

When Belshazzar's body was found, he suspected that it had to be either the good reverend or his son. He had heard in town that Belshazzar had his way with little Abigail Hancock, not that he gave a damn. He hated the Hancocks. To his way of thinking, Negroes were inferior and were born to be made slaves, and any white person who said otherwise was trash. As far as trash went, Reverend Hancock was on the top of Sheriff Jones' list. He hated John Allen and his family just as much, because of their friendship with the Hancocks. The problem was, Sheriff Jones was afraid of both the good reverend and John Allen. Mainly because both had fought in the War of 1812 and Jones himself had seen the reverend in a brawl or two, before and after he became a minister. But now that he had the whole town with him, he wasn't as scared. He still didn't know which Hancock killed his boy, whether it was the father or son, but he was going to find out and would not rest until one or both of them had a rope around his neck.

As he and his posse rode on the plantation, they were immediately stopped by John Allen Jr. and William Allen who, along with ten of their field slaves, were armed. "What can we do for you, Sheriff," asked John Jr.

"Is your pa home?"

"I am right here, Frederick," answered John Sr. as he stepped out onto the porch, also armed with his musket. Behind him came Nehemiah, who was unarmed. He stood beside his friend and saw a look of hatred in the eyes of the sheriff. Jones stared coldly at Nehemiah with murder in his eyes.

"You know why I am here, Allen, and I think your nigger-loving preacher friend knows why, too."

"I heard about Belshazzar, Frederick," said John Sr. "You have our deepest condolences."

"Like Hell you do!" John Allen never called Jones by his title, feeling that he didn't deserve to be a sheriff or in any position of authority.

Frederick Jones knew this, and it irritated him. "Where were you last night, Reverend?"

"My wife and I were here last night, attending to our daughter," said Nehemiah. "After your son brutally raped and beat her near to death."

Jones nearly lost his temper and was about to go for his pistol, but then thought better of it when he realized that he and his posse were outgunned.

"That is a very serious accusation, Reverend Hancock," said Tom Hooper. Hooper was a local blacksmith and also didn't care much for the Hancocks, but he wasn't too fond of the sheriff, either. Since he had a daughter himself, he didn't have much sympathy for Belshazzar Jones getting blown away, if what he heard was true. "Do you have any proof that young Belshazzar raped your daughter?"

"You can ask her yourself when she is better," said Nehemiah. "She told us that Belshazzar attacked her on her way home from town yesterday morning, and John's sons and one of his slaves found her by the creek, nearly dead."

"That is a damned lie and you know it, you nigger-loving son of bitch!" shouted Sheriff Jones. "Everybody knows that your little girl is probably a whore who likes it rough!"

That was more than young Jason Allen would tolerate. "Your son deserved what he got!"

"Jason, be quiet," said John Sr. "Look here, Frederick. If Little Abigail Hancock said that your boy raped her, then he raped her. Now my question is, what is the reason for your presence on my property?"

"I want my son's killer, and if the good reverend here is not the killer, he knows who is."

"You're right about one thing, Frederick Jones," said Nehemiah. "I did not kill your son, but I sure wish I did."

"What about *your* son, Azariah?" asked Tom Hooper. "Do you know where he was last night, and better yet, is he here?"

Before Nehemiah could answer, John answered for him. "He is not here."

"Forgive me if I don't take your word for it, Allen," said Jones sarcastically. "Surely you won't mind if we search your fine plantation."

Allen and his boys, as well as their armed slaves, raised their muskets at the posse. Jason Allen had his musket pointing straight at the sheriff. "I do mind," said John. "This is my home, my property, and you have no authority here. Jones, with that being said, you and your lynch mob have until the count of ten to get the hell off, before you join your son."

Frederick Jones and his men knew that this was a battle they would lose. The Allen family had connections and were powerful in Montgomery County, another reason why Frederick Jones hated them so much. But there was little he could do about it now. "This ain't over, John Allen, and you, nigger-loving preacher, you better watch your back. I will find your boy, one way or another, and he will hang, that I promise you!"

5

"Azariah is going to have to leave here," said Nehemiah. Mother Abigail was stunned. The good reverend and his wife, along with John Allen, Champ, and some of the other servants were in the barn, helping Azariah out of the hole they had him hidden in.

"And just where is he supposed to go?" asked his mother. "He is only fourteen, for God's sake!"

"Fourteen and already has a death sentence on his head," said John. "Nehemiah is right. If Azariah stays, the sheriff and his friends will find him and hang him the first chance they get, without trial."

"I know where to go, Mother," said Azariah. "I thought about it, right after I sent Belshazzar Jones straight to hell. I'll go west."

Everyone looked at the boy with renewed curiosity. "Just how far west?" asked his father.

"Past St. Louis, Missouri."

John Allen was both surprised and impressed. "That far, huh?"

"But there is nothing out west past St. Louis, except wild vermin, ruffians and red Indians," said mother Abigail. "Son, I am told that they will kill you as soon as they just look at you."

"Mother, it is not like I have much of a choice now, do I?"

responded Azariah. "I would rather take my chances out where Lewis and Clark have traveled than stay here and end up with a rope around my neck."

Azariah's mother was about to say more, but her husband stopped her. "Our son is right, Abigail. No matter how much it hurts us, he has a better chance out west than staying here."

Tears welled up in Abigail as she gave in. Azariah hugged both of his parents, while John had Champ and the other servants prepare a horse for him. A little while later, around midnight, Alice had Mabel bring cornbread, hardtack, and two canteens of water to the farm for Azariah's travel. Azariah still had his father's blunderbuss that he used to kill Belshazzar. His father carried that weapon with him all through the War of 1812, while he was in the army. Azariah was about to give it back to him, but his father decided to let him keep it. John Allen provided Azariah with a Pennsylvania rifle, along with two powder horns and a butcher knife. Allen also gave the boy five hundred dollars for his journey. Satisfied with everything, Azariah was ready to go.

"It is time," he said.

"Wait," said Abigail. She quickly ran back to the main house and returned with a Bible. "I want you to have this, Son. We don't know where you are going or how far, but just remember the Lord is with you always."

Azariah was hesitant to take it, but his father strongly urged him to. "I know what you are feeling, Son. I have felt it many times. But your mother is right. Wherever you are going, you must not forget who your God is, and you must keep Him with you and let Him guide your path."

Azariah took the Bible and put it in his saddlebag. "Tell Little Abigail that I love her, and I will never forget any of you." With those last words, Azariah rode off the Allen plantation and into the middle of the night, saying goodbye to Maryland. It was the beginning of spring in mid-March of the year 1820.

6

_____

A few weeks later, near Lawrenceburg, Tennessee, twelve-year-old John Wesley Crockett, along with his younger siblings and half-siblings, had just completed their chores on the family farm and were washing up when their father, the famous frontiersman and veteran of the War of 1812, Davey Crockett, got home from work.

"Get your schooling done today, boys?" he asked John and his younger brother, William, who was eleven.

"We sure did, Pa!"

"Was it fun?" The boys shook their heads. The former frontiersman and Indian fighter laughed. "Great. Money well spent," he said.

Since the war ended almost six years previously, the native Tennessean, who preferred to be called David instead of Davey, managed to start several successful businesses while raising a family and working as the Justice of the Peace. Additionally, for the past two years, he was head of the 57th Regiment of the Tennessee Militia as their lieutenant colonel. During those years, however, he suffered a tragedy. His first wife, Polly, who was the mother of John, William, and their sister Margaret, died nearly five years previously. However,

David would remarry a few months later to Elizabeth Patton, a widow, and he would raise her two children, George and Margaret Ann, as his own.

Like his first marriage, his second one was happy. David and Elizabeth welcomed a son, Robert, who would be three in September, and a daughter, Rebecca, who would be two in December. When he wasn't with his family or doing his duties as a public servant, David was running what was probably his most successful business that helped provide for his family—the water-powered grist mill. He also ran a powder mill and distillery on Shoal Creek. However, those who knew the man knew he preferred to spend time with his family. Not having a close relationship with his father, David Crockett was determined to be a better father to his children than his father was to him. It bothered him greatly that his businesses and his public service duties often kept him away from his family, so anytime he was home, he made it a priority to spend time with his wife and children as much as possible.

While Elizabeth was getting dinner ready, David sat in his favorite rocking chair and had both Robert and Rebecca on his lap. He was about to read them a story from the Bible, when seven-year-old Margaret tapped on his shoulder, trying to get her father's attention. "Someone is coming up the road, Pa."

"Oh," he said. Knowing the family didn't usually get visitors, despite the reputation of the patriarch, David thought it strange that someone would visit his homestead just when the sun was setting.

John and William were already at the door and saw the stranger on horseback riding towards them. "He's a huge one, Pa," said William. "Should we get the rifles?"

"Hold that thought," said David.

David Crockett was a devout Christian and a kind-hearted human being, but he was no fool. Despite his reputation as an Indian fighter, he did not hate Indians. He was one of the few white people who did not care about skin color and was also a staunch opponent of the mistreatment of American Indians. This of course earned him some enemies, one of them another Tennessean named General Andrew Jackson, under whom Crockett served during the War of 1812. David watched as the stranger rode to a stop in front of his home. The man was huge, probably taller than Crockett himself, who was no little person.

"Greetings, sir," said the stranger. After hearing his voice, Crockett couldn't help but be shocked. This was still a young boy, probably no older than John himself.

"How do you do, young man?"

"Tired and hungry, sir," answered the stranger. "My name is Azariah Hancock, and I have come a long way."

David sensed that the boy was no threat to his family, and he did look famished.

"Well, come on down," David said. "Tonight is your lucky night; my wife was just getting dinner ready."

"Thank you, sir," said Azariah as he got off his horse. "I am sorry, mister, but I didn't catch your name."

"David Crockett at your service, but some folks in these parts call me Davey."

Azariah's eyes widened in shock and awe. He had heard of the exploits of the famous Davey Crockett from his father, and now he was standing before the legend himself, shaking his hand.

The frontiersman was amused. "Relax, son. You're only looking at a man, not Jesus Christ Himself."

"My father served in the war against the British at Horseshoe Bend. I wonder if you knew him."

"What was his name?"

"Nehemiah Hancock," said Azariah. "He is a preacher now."

"I see," said David. "How old are you, Azariah?"

"I just turned fourteen this past January first."

"Fourteen!" exclaimed David. "You look like you're at least thirty!" David Crockett couldn't get over the fact that Azariah was extremely tall for his age. However, he also sensed that the young boy was either hiding something or running from something or both.

"Well, why don't you come on in?" he said as he introduced Azariah to his family. "These are my eldest boys, John and William, and my daughter, Margaret."

Azariah shook hands with the older Crockett children and was quickly introduced to George and Margaret Ann as well as the babies, Robert and Rebecca. Elizabeth brought dinner to the table after the introductions were made. During dinner, David and Elizabeth noticed that it was probably a while since Azariah had had a decent meal. After dinner and when he was more relaxed, they decided to break the ice.

"Mrs. Crockett, that was the best meal I have had in a long while," said Azariah.

"Why, thank you."

"Tell us, Azariah," said David. "Where are you from?"

"Maryland, sir."

"That is a long way from Tennessee, don't you think?" said Elizabeth.

David noticed that Azariah was getting uncomfortable and decided to send the children to bed. It was getting late anyway. "You're not in trouble with the law, are you, son?"

Azariah gave the former frontiersman a look that confirmed his suspicions. "Yes, sir, I am." Seeing no reason to lie, Azariah explained what happened to his sister and why he was forced to leave his home and his family.

The Crocketts believed every word, and David strongly sympathized with the young man. "What you did was very brave, Azariah. Not many good men would get justice for their sister in face of injustice."

"I am not sure it was justice that I was looking for Mr. Crockett," said Azariah. "It feels more like vengeance."

David raised an eyebrow and smiled. "In your case, they go hand in hand."

"How so?" asked Azariah.

"From what you told me, this Belshazzar Jones person was the son of the sheriff and nephew of the county judge, who both hated your family because of your strong opposition towards slavery. Since it was obvious that your sister was not going to get justice on that reason alone, you had no choice but to take matters into your own hands."

Azariah pondered that for a moment. "You think so?"

David nodded. "Now if Belshazzar was going to be arrested for raping your sister and given a fair trial, that would have been a different story, but since we both know that was not going to happen, I would have to say you did the right thing."

"It is getting late," said Elizabeth. "Azariah, why don't you stay with us for a while?"

Azariah was not sure if that was a good idea. For all he knew, there could already be a bounty on his head, even though he was already hundreds of miles from Maryland. Plus, he didn't want to bring any trouble upon the Crockett family, not after the kindness they had shown him. "I do not want to be a burden unto you and your family, ma'am."

"No burden at all," said Elizabeth. "Plus, we could use some extra help around the farm."

"And you will be paid for it," added David. "You will also be safe with us, so you can stay as long as you like."

Since he was in no rush, Azariah decided to take the Crocketts up on their offer.

7

For almost two months, Azariah lived and worked for the Crockett family. He became a surrogate big brother for the Crockett children, even though he was only two years older than John Crockett. But on the first day of June, he was getting worried and restless. Worried, because he could not shake the feeling that he was still being hunted, and he was afraid he would bring nothing but trouble to the Crockett family. Restless, because he planned to head west towards the wilderness, past St. Louis to the Rocky Mountains, where Lewis and Clark explored two years before his birth. Later that night, he informed David and Elizabeth Crockett that he was moving on.

Although both were sad to see him go, they understood. "I was a lot like you when I was your age, Azariah," said David. "Wanting to see what was beyond the next horizon."

"I am happy and grateful for what you and Mrs. Crockett have done for me this past couple of months," said Azariah. "But I am still wanted for murder back in Maryland, and I don't wish to take the chance of bounty hunters showing up on your doorstep, looking for me and putting your loved ones in danger. I could not live with myself if that ever happened."

"We understand, Azariah," said Elizabeth. "Our children will miss you very much, especially John and William. You three have become close since you arrived."

"Ma'am, I never had the pleasure of having a little brother or sister, so I guess being close to them was not that difficult for me."

"When will you leave?" asked David.

"First thing in the morning, sir."

"Good. We will have an extra horse, some food, as well as some supplies for your journey," said David.

"You don't have to do that, sir," responded Azariah.

But David would not be put off. "Nonsense. The Good Lord in His Holy Word said it is better to give than it is to receive. You have worked for everything you deserve, so I will hear no more of it."

"Just remember to say goodbye to the children before you leave in the morning," said Elizabeth.

"I will, ma'am."

Before calling it a night, David Crockett and Azariah sat outside on the front porch for a while. "Azariah, before you leave in the morning, there is one thing I would like to tell you, something that a good man should live by always."

"What is that, sir?" asked Azariah.

David Crockett paused for a moment and then answered, "Before you make a decision, make sure it is the right one, then go on ahead."

———

Three weeks later in St. Louis, Missouri, Irish trapper Liam O'Reilly sat by a fireplace in a tavern not far from the docks. He arrived in St. Louis from the Rocky Mountains a few days previously to sell his plews. Beaver plews sold up to six dollars a pound in St. Louis, more than they did at the many trading posts up and down the frontier where trappers such as O'Reilly had no choice but to sell them for less than that. Despite having a strong dislike for the still-growing city of St. Louis, O'Reilly often made the long travel from the west into town to sell his plews from both his winter and spring trapping seasons for better prices. However, doing so was dangerous. Traveling from the Rocky Mountains took weeks—sometimes months—especially when a man had heavily laden pack mules or pack horses. Trappers, or mountain men as they were better known, dealt with unpredictable weather, accidents, even more—unpredictable wild animals, such as grizzly bears, wolverines, mountain lions, and packs of wolves, not to mention countless of American Indian tribes that roamed the west. Some were friendly to the mountain men; others were not.

Most, if not all, the tribes, both friendly and hostile, considered the white men to be invaders, and rightfully so. After all, Indians had been living up and down the plains and the mountains from the Mississippi River all the way to California since time immemorial. Suddenly white men started coming into their land around the mid-1600s. They were coming from the north from Canada and from the south from Mexico. Lewis and Clark showing up from the east around 1804-1805 were just the latest.

At first, white men came to trade and trap beaver for the pelts. That was not a problem for the tribes initially. But once the invaders started bringing alcohol and hurting and attacking Indian women, the relationship between trappers and traders and the tribes started to unravel. The inevitable introduction of smallpox made things a lot worse. However, despite these problems, the relationship between the American Indian tribes and the white men, at least in the case of the mountain men, was not too big of a problem compared to the later decades in which more and more settlers were coming. The fur trade years were probably the most peaceful times between Indians and non-Indians alike because there were not many non-Indians other than trappers like Liam O'Reilly living in the Rocky Mountains. They made up less than two percent of the population west of the Mississippi River during the summer of 1820.

Hostile Indians were not the only problems trappers faced. The biggest threat that trappers faced was each other. American Indians at least were more honest when it came to who they liked, disliked, or trusted. Nothing got a trapper killed more quickly than his racial ignorance. Many a lone white man who came across another white man or group of white men in the Rockies paid the ultimate price when they thought that just because a stranger was of the same skin color that he was safe. No man was more savage than a white man.

This was something Liam O'Reilly was taught by his friend and mentor, the late John Colter. The thirty-year-old Irishman arrived in St. Louis when he was fifteen, back in 1805. He met the famous mountain man a year later while traveling up the Mississippi with two other greenhorn trappers. Colter had just been discharged from the Corps of Discovery by Lewis and Clark and took a liking to the Irish teenager.

Liam learned a lot from Colter, and he also learned that he loved trapping and hunting and living among the Indians. One tribe in particular was the Northern Cheyenne. While working for the Missouri Fur Company in 1809, Liam was hunting near the Powder River at the mouth of the Yellowstone, near modern-day Terry, Montana. He brought down a full-grown cow elk and was about to skin and gut it when a deadly wolverine came by and challenged the nineteen-year-old mountain man for his prize.

O'Reilly won the battle with a perfect thrust to the beast's belly, but not before the animal took a chunk from his right side. While trying to stop the blood flow before it got infected or he bled to death, a Cheyenne hunting party passed by and found him. They not only managed to heal him but put him on a travois and took him and the elk and wolverine carcasses back to their village. It was there his life changed forever, at least according to him.

O'Reilly learned the Cheyenne tongue through the universal sign language that trappers and Indians used to communicate with each other. He had hunted with them and even helped to fight their enemies the Crow, Blackfeet, and the Ute. In 1814, he fell in love with a sixteen-year-old Cheyenne girl named Rain Cloud and gave her father twenty horses for her hand in marriage, which the father accepted graciously. Liam and his bride moved deep into the Beartooth Mountains, where they lived in a cabin that he had built for them a few months before, while they were courting. The marriage was a happy one, with the birth of their daughter, Constance, in February of 1815, during a visit to the Cheyenne.

However, tragedy struck, that summer in June to be exact. While he was hunting, a Crow war party attacked the cabin and murdered Rain Cloud and the baby. When Liam came back and found his wife and daughter murdered, he hunted down the war party. By the time he reached them, he counted ten of them—nine adult warriors and a young boy possibly on his first war attack. Liam was filled with rage and a thirst for vengeance and attacked the war party armed with two muskets, four pistols, and two Cheyenne tomahawks. He waded through them like a berserker. He successfully killed all of them except the young boy. He was wounded in the process but not badly.

Despite what they did to his wife and child, Liam could not bring himself to kill a boy, so he spared him and told him to tell all Crows that that day they made an enemy of him. The boy nodded and was allowed to flee, but not before giving Liam the name Raging Bull. The name stuck with him from that fateful day on.

After taking the heads of the adult Crow warriors and burying his wife and infant daughter, O'Reilly left the mountains and went to the summer camp of his adopted people to find his in-laws and mourn with them over the loss of Rain Cloud and the baby.

Five years to the day later, the Irishman sat in a tavern, thinking about Rain Cloud and Constance. Knowing that the life of a trapper was dangerous and that living in the wilderness at the edge of the world was also dangerous didn't diminish Liam's pain. He enjoyed the company of his in-laws when he visited them during the late spring and early summer months before going to St. Louis to sell his plews, but since the death of Rain Cloud, he always felt an emptiness. She was so much in his thoughts, he didn't notice the voluptuous Spanish barmaid who approached him while he was sitting by the fireplace in the tavern.

"Could you use some company?"

The Irishman slowly looked up at the lady. He was impressed by her tan skin and black hair. She had a seductive smile along with ample cleavage that seemed burst out of her low-cut dress. She appeared to him to be at least in her mid- to late-twenties, so she was no child. Finding no reason to be alone, he invited her to sit. She graciously accepted.

"I haven't seen you around here, have I?" she asked in her thick Spanish accent.

Liam gave a handsome smile and slowly shook his head. "I don't come to St. Louis much," he said in his Irish brogue. "Last time I was in this tavern was fourteen years ago."

"Dios mio!" exclaimed the woman. "What brings you back?"

O'Reilly just shrugged. "Life is too short, I guess, so I thought I would come and visit to see how much the place has changed."

"Maria is my name," said the barmaid, offering her hand.

The trapper gently shook it. "Liam O'Reilly."

"Where are you from, Liam?"

"Born in Dublin, Ireland, but I was raised in Boston, Massachusetts, before coming out here back in '05."

Maria was curious. By the way Liam was dressed, she could tell that he was a trapper and that was probably why he came out west that long ago. In her line of work, many of her customers were trappers and mountain men who came back and forth to sell their plews to make their fortune. Most of those who went out into the unknown never returned, more than likely killed. "Do you come from the wilderness out west?" she asked.

"Aye."

"What's it like?"

Liam thought for a moment, then smiled. "It is the Garden of Eden or close to it."

"You must love it, to venture out there as long as you have," said Maria.

"I do," responded Liam. "I have kin out there. Well, more like in-laws, but kin none the same." For a moment, Liam thought he saw the disappointment in Maria's eyes.

"You're married," she remarked.

Liam turned back to the fire and sighed for a moment. "I was."

Maria realized she touched a sore spot. "I am sorry, Señor Liam. I did not know you are a widower."

"No apologies necessary," he said.

It was quiet for a moment, but then Liam asked Maria something no man had ever asked her. "How come you never married?"

Maria was surprised by the question. "Women like me don't get married, at least not to decent gentlemen."

"I disagree," said Liam. "You seem intelligent as well as beautiful enough to find a decent gentleman to sink your claws into."

Maria giggled and blushed when she realized that the trapper just paid her a compliment. For the next hour or so, they talked. The more they talked, the more Maria found herself liking the trapper and even invited him to spend the night with her in her room free of charge. However, Liam respectfully declined.

"Nothing against you, lass," he said. "The only woman who I have been with is... was my dear wife, may God rest her soul, and I am not ready for that again." Maria looked at him in the eyes and could tell that he was telling the truth. "Well, I better get a move on," said Liam. "The Rockies await. Oh, here is ten dollars for the company. It has been greatly appreciated."

"Gracias!"

As he stood, Maria didn't realize how tall the Irishman was—probably six-foot-four and weighing a good two hundred and seventy pounds of muscle. Not to mention, he was extremely handsome for a trapper.

"You sure you don't want to stay?" she asked.

Liam just smiled at her and nodded as he slowly turned and

picked up his rifle and wolverine hat. He gently bowed to Maria before walking off into the summer afternoon.

As he left the tavern, he accidentally bumped into a much taller and larger man who wasn't paying attention to where he was going.

"Sorry, sir," said the stranger.

O'Reilly was shocked after hearing the stranger's voice. He quickly realized that the stranger was still a teenager but looked like a full-grown man.

"No harm is done, lad," he said. "You must be new in town."

"You could say that," said the stranger. "You know where I can find a place to eat?"

O'Reilly raised his thumb and pointed to the tavern he just came out of. "Tell me, lad, how old are you?"

"Fourteen, sir," said the stranger.

Liam gasped. "Fourteen! You look like you're at least thirty!"

The stranger laughed. "You are the second person to say that to me."

"Oh, who was the first?"

"David Crockett."

Liam was about to guffaw, then stopped when he realized the young boy was not joshing him. He had heard of the famous frontiersman, but only a few who lived outside the state of Tennessee ever met him. "You serious, lad? You met *the* Davey Crockett?"

"Met him?" said the stranger. "I lived with him and his family for almost two months."

"Bloody hell!" exclaimed Liam. "Liam O'Reilly is my name."

Liam extended his towards the young man, who accepted and shook it.

"Azariah Hancock."

"What brings you to St. Louis, Azariah?"

Azariah paused for a moment, not sure if he wanted to tell Liam the real reason. But after looking at the Irishman's gentle demeanor and the clothes he was wearing, so typical of the trappers and mountain men that lived out west, he saw no reason to lie.

"I am heading out west to become a trapper."

Liam raised an eyebrow. "Are you now?"

Azariah just nodded. He wasn't sure if he liked Liam's suspicious expression. At the same time, there was something about the man that said he was not a threat.

"Aren't you kind of young for such dangerous work?" asked Liam.

"Maybe, maybe not," responded Azariah. "But it is not like I have much of a choice."

Liam did not need to ask what the youth meant by that. Most trappers who came out west were either runaway teenagers who escaped from an abusive home or apprenticeship, or fugitives from the law, and since there was no law west of the Mississippi River during the 1820s, the wilderness and the Rocky Mountains were the closest things to true freedom they would ever have.

Most of the black trappers were runaway slaves who fled plantations in Missouri, Tennessee, and Kentucky. Very few black trappers like the famous (or infamous) Edward Rose were free men of color. Liam O'Reilly had met and befriended many trappers both white and black, however, Rose was not among those friends. The majority of the people that he considered his true and closest friends were Indians, mostly from his adopted tribe, the Northern Cheyenne and their allies, the Northern Arapahoe and the Lakota. However, there was something about Azariah that Liam took a liking to. He couldn't pinpoint it and decided to not express it until both he and the young lad were comfortable with each other.

"You hungry, lad?"

"Starving," answered Azariah. "I have some money to pay for my dinner, so you don't have to go through all the trouble."

"Really?" asked Liam, again with a raised eyebrow.

"I didn't steal it," said Azariah. "If that is what you are suggesting."

"Not at all, lad," answered Liam. "But if I was you, I wouldn't go announcing that you have money here in St. Louis."

"Why?"

"Because a lad of your age with enough money in his pockets to buy his dinner or more will attract the wrong attention," answered Liam. "From both the law and from those who break the law." Azariah understood and filed that advice in the back of his head. Knowing that he understood, Liam patted Azariah on the shoulder and invited him inside the tavern. "Come along, lad. Let's fill your meat bag."

The two entered the tavern and sat down at a table by the entrance. Azariah looked Liam up and down and automatically figured that he was someone that you didn't trifle with. He also noticed the scar that lined his left cheek as if he had been in a knife fight. Other than that, Liam was almost as tall as he was, and he noticed that they both had red hair. Azariah's mother was a red-headed woman and he inherited that, while his twin sister inherited their father's blond hair. Liam signaled Maria over to the table, who was happy to see him return so quickly.

"Back so soon, Liam?" she asked.

Liam just laughed and introduced Azariah.

"Pleasure to meet you," Maria said.

"Likewise, ma'am."

"Maria, can you get us the best steaks you got?" asked Liam.

"Of course," answered Maria. "Anything to drink?"

"Water for me," answered Liam. "You, Azariah?"

"The same. Water."

Some of the other patrons in the tavern overheard and snickered. No one had ever heard of a trapper in a tavern drinking water over whiskey or anything that contained alcohol. They were also surprised that since Liam was Irish, he hadn't consumed anything but water since he got there. However, Liam, Azariah, and Maria paid them no mind. Maria went away to fill their orders while the men got to know each other better.

"So, lad," said Liam, "you never told me why you want to be a trapper." Azariah wasn't sure if he should tell Liam the entire truth, but Liam sensed his distrust. "This is just between you and me, lad," he promised. "Not even sweet Maria has to know."

Sensing that he could be trusted, Azariah quietly told the Irishman everything, from his twin sister's rape to ending the life of the son of bitch who raped her and why he had to flee his Maryland home, leaving behind his family and what few friends he did have. He told him of how he met David Crockett and his family and stayed with them for a couple of months before leaving for here.

"I heard that out west a man can start a new beginning, without worrying about his past catching up to him."

"Aye, lad," said Liam. "This is true, but it comes at a price." Liam was about to explain the ways of a trapper to Azariah when Maria returned with their meals and glasses of water. Liam paid Maria generously more than the meals cost, for which she was grateful and she let him know, before returning to her work.

Azariah noticed how pretty she was and even mentioned as much to Liam. "I think she likes you."

"Maybe," responded Liam. "You never know, though, when it comes to the ladies in her profession."

Despite his youth, Azariah understood what the Irishman meant by that. "She's not a...?"

"Aye, lad," answered Liam with a grin. "She is."

Azariah turned red as he chopped into a steak. Wanting to change the subject, he asked Liam more questions about being a trapper.

"You serious about going west and becoming a trapper, eh?" asked Liam. Azariah just nodded. "Well, I will tell you that it is not for weaklings," said Liam. "It is constant backbreaking work, trapping for beaver." Azariah listened intently as the Irishman continued to explain. "There are two trapping seasons—the fall season and the spring season—and in both cases, the lakes and rivers where trappers go to trap beaver are freezing, or it feels that way sometimes."

"Is it worth it?" asked Azariah.

"Aye, lad," answered Liam. "As long as uppity rich people are still buying beaver hats in New York, London, Paris, and even here in St. Louis, a trapper can make up to almost five thousand dollars a year, sometimes up to ten thousand."

Azariah almost choked as he was swallowing water from his cup, hearing how much money a man could make from trapping. "That much in a year?"

"If he lives long enough," answered Liam. "And is smart with his money." Azariah again was looking at the scar running down Liam's left cheek. "Crow did that to me," said Liam.

"Huh?"

The Irishman smiled. "The scar on my cheek," he said. "A Crow warrior trying to take my scalp a few years back did this to me."

"Must've been one hell of a fight," said Azariah.

"Aye, lad, it was," answered Liam. "But I came out on top." Liam then showed Azariah the scalp of the Crow warrior hanging from his belt.

"Good Heavens," said Azariah as he touched it. "What are they like out there? Indians, I mean."

"Human beings just like us, lad," said Liam. "Some are good, some bad, but the reason I have lasted as long as I have compared to most trappers is that I respect them."

"Even the bad Indians?" asked Azariah. "But why?"

"Simple, lad. They were here first long before any of us came," answered Liam. "You have to look at it from their point of view. We are invaders, at least to some of the tribes." Liam paused for a moment and took a sip of water from his cup. "Even tribes who are friendly to the trappers don't fully trust them and for good reason."

"Which is?" asked Azariah.

"We come into their land and take from it, without giving back, abuse their women, and in some cases, bring a plague of smallpox down on them by giving them infected blankets."

Azariah was not completely surprised at what he was hearing, considering where he came from and grew up. He knew that white men did not have the most diplomatic way of meeting and respecting people who were different from them. But still, he found it a tad bit hard to believe what Liam was telling him. "You sure you are not exaggerating a bit?"

"Nope," answered Liam. "I have seen it done myself and it is no wonder a lot of them either don't like or trust us."

"How long have you lived out west?" asked Azariah.

"Going on fourteen years now, thereabouts."

"If it is that bad, then why do you stay?"

Liam smiled. "Freedom, lad," he answered. "I learned a long time ago that there is more to a man's life than money and that is freedom." Liam paused for a second to think. "When I was about eighteen years old, I was in my second year going into my third year as a free trapper in the Rocky Mountains." He paused again as he reminisced. "It was me and John Colter who trapped up and down the Yellowstone and beyond," he said. "By this time, we had both made enough money from selling our beaver plews to live like kings here in St. Louis, but every year we stayed in the mountains to trap and explore, looking for what was over the next hill."

"Sounds like an adventure," said Azariah.

"It is, lad," responded Liam. "Then Manuel Lisa comes and starts the Missouri Fur Company back in '09, and I and John decide to trap for him and sell our plews to his company, instead of returning to St. Louis every year." Liam stopped again to take another sip of water and a bite of his steak. When he was done, he continued. "It is around that time I was living among the Cheyenne Indians, who often resided near the Powder River region."

"What are they like?" asked Azariah.

Liam smiled as he put the explanation together in his head. "Proud and wonderful people," he said. "Don't get me wrong—they can be fierce as any warrior tribe when they are provoked—but for me, you would not meet a more honest and honorable people than them, besides their friends, the Arapahoe and the Lakota."

"You married?" asked Azariah. Liam gave the youth a slight look that troubled him. Azariah took it as a sign that he may have touched a nerve. "I meant no offense," he said.

"I know you didn't, lad," said Liam. "One of the key lessons about being a trapper is to be careful when it comes to asking questions about one's personal life."

"I understand," said Azariah as he returned to eating.

"Now, to answer your question. Yes, I was married," said Liam. "I am widowed now."

"I am sorry to hear that."

"Appreciate it."

After both had finished their meal, Liam and Azariah took a walk outside the tavern. The sun had just set over St. Louis, and Liam was planning on getting ready for his journey back to the mountains the next day. He contemplated taking Azariah with him and training him to become a trapper and mountain man. "Do you still wish to become a trapper and move west, lad?"

"Absolutely," answered Azariah. "I would consider it an honor if you took me with you and taught me how."

Liam was flattered and had secretly decided that he was going to take the youth with him anyway. He liked Azariah, and knowing his story, admired his grit. Plus, Azariah would not only be safe under his tutelage but far, far, far from the grasp of the law. "I was planning on leaving tomorrow, lad, but since you wish to come with me, that means you will need supplies and new clothes for the journey."

"What is wrong with the clothes that I have on now?" asked Azariah.

Liam chuckled. "Where we are going, you won't last a winter in the mountains or the plains without proper clothing."

Azariah looked at his clothes. They were good for living on a farm, but then he looked at how Liam was dressed. He wore a buckskin shirt and pants that were highly decorated with beads from top to bottom. He even wore moccasins that looked like they were more comfortable to walk in than the boots he was wearing.

"Don't fret, lad," said Liam. "Tomorrow, we will get you a new coat, at least, that will sustain you for winter. Your rifles seem okay, but you need supplies and some extra ammo."

"What about the clothes that you wear?" asked Azariah.

"They don't sell them here in St. Louis," answered Liam. "Again, don't fret. Where we are going, you will have a brand new buckskin shirt and pants made for you in no time."

"I am grateful for this, Liam," said Azariah. "I promise I will give you my one hundred and ten percent best, and I will not let you down."

The Irishman smiled at the young man's confidence. "Of that, lad, I have no doubt. I think we are going to be excellent partners."

8

Three weeks later, the duo was following the Mississippi River. They had left St. Louis two days after they met, and they had just passed what would be known as modern-day Independence, Missouri a week previously. They were now entering Omaha country when they spotted their first herd of buffalo. Azariah, who was riding his brand new black stallion that Liam bought for him back in St. Louis, gawked in awe at the shaggy beasts. The horse that he rode from Maryland, a brown stallion, had now become one of the two new pack horses he acquired thanks to his new mentor. He also bought a brand new Hudson Bay red and yellow mackinaw coat. However, he did not wear it yet, because it was still summer, nearing the end of June to be exact.

Once they saw the herd, Azariah became astonished. He had heard about the shaggy beasts that were three times the size of a horse, but he had to see it to believe it. Now that he was seeing for the first time, he was completely awestruck.

"Magnificent, aren't they?" said Liam.

"They're beautiful."

The Irishman snickered. He remembered his reaction when he

first came out west and saw his first herd of buffalo. "They're delicious too," he said. "To most of the tribes out here, the buffalo is more than just food."

"Oh?" said Azariah. "What else are they used for?"

"Just about everything," answered Liam. "Nothing on the buffalo goes to waste. Their hide makes great blankets, their stomachs are often used as containers, and many of the body parts are used for a variety of things that are needed." Liam called to a halt and signaled Azariah to slowly step down.

"What are we doing?"

"Hunting," answered Liam. "Nothing satisfies this coon's belly like fresh buffalo meat, especially the ribs, liver, and tongue."

It was clear to Azariah that they were going to be there for a while, so he and Liam set up camp near the river a mile from the herd. Then they got their rifles and pack horses and slowly rode up to the herd. Liam silently told Azariah to watch him first, and then follow his example.

Azariah was an apt student. He watched as the Irish trapper loaded his Pennsylvania rifle, took aim, and fired. In a split second, he brought down a full-grown buffalo cow. Azariah was both amazed and relieved that the herd appeared unconcerned with the downed female. He was afraid that they might stampede from the gunshot. He realized that would not be the case once Liam reloaded and quickly fired his rifle again, bringing down a bull this time.

"All right, lad," said Liam. "Your turn."

Azariah obliged and loaded his Pennsylvania rifle, which was one of two rifles that he owned. The other was his father's blunderbuss. Carefully repeating the action of his mentor, Azariah picked the closest animal, which turned out to be a full-grown bull, aimed and fired. The beast when down, convulsing after being hit. Liam patted the youth on his back, congratulating him.

"That was something, lad," said Liam. "Now see if you can shoot a cow next."

"Does it matter if I shoot a bull or cow?" asked Azariah.

Liam nodded. "Aye, lad. Buffalo cows have more meat on them than the bulls and taste better too."

With that information, Azariah picked out a lone cow that had strayed a little far from the herd. After reloading, he repeated the process and fired. The cow was down in a split second.

"That is enough, lad," said Liam. "Now it is time to make meat."

For the rest of the day, the duo skinned, gutted, and butchered all four animals, using the pack horses to drag the meat-laden travois they had made back to camp. Nothing was wasted. Azariah watched and learned as Liam cracked open each skull with his tomahawk and took out the brains and put them in a pouch that he learned was made from the stomach of a buffalo.

"What are the brains for?" asked Azariah.

"For tanning the hides," answered Liam. "Indian women use them for that. It makes the hide usable to keep a body warm during the cold months." While he was taking out the insides of the last buffalo he had shot, Azariah looked up to see Liam chewing on one of the livers.

Liam offered it to the youth, but Azariah wasn't sure if he was up to it.

"Try it, lad," said Liam. "Nothing warms a belly than raw buffalo liver."

"But it is not cooked," said Azariah.

"Doesn't matter, lad. It is not going to hurt," said Liam. "Go on, take a bite."

Azariah reluctantly took a bite and his expression changed.

"Well?" asked Liam. "What do you think?"

"Tastes better than chicken," said Azariah. "Tastes better than cattle meat, for that matter, too."

By the time they were done and returned to camp with all the meat that they needed, it was almost dark. Azariah got the fire started and quickly put some of the meat on a spit. Liam got out the coffee and went to the river to fill their canteens and the coffee pot. After they finished their dinner, Liam and Azariah checked on their rifles and pistols to see that they were cleaned and loaded. After the inspection and assured that the weapons were primed, Azariah went to check on the horses, while Liam helped himself to some more coffee. As the animals grazed on the grass where they were hobbled, Azariah rubbed them down and gave them some apples he brought from St. Louis as a treat.

Satisfied the animals were secure, he returned to camp and found Liam smoking a pipe, humming. "Liam?"

"Hmm?" answered the Irishman.

"Can I ask you a question?"

"I don't see why not."

"It might be personal," said Azariah.

Liam just smiled. "Don't worry, lad. If I feel you're invading my personal life, I will let you know."

"What made you come out west?"

"Interesting question," said Liam. "To be honest with you, lad, I just got sick and tired of living in Boston, I guess."

Azariah was a little surprised. "I thought you were from Ireland?"

"Aye, I am," said Liam. "But my family and I moved to Boston when I was ten years old."

"How many brothers and sisters do you have?"

"I am the sixth of eight children," answered Liam. "Five boys and three girls."

Azariah thought for a moment. "That is a big family," he said. "Do you miss them?"

Liam snickered. "Hell, no," he said. "Don't get me wrong. I love my parents and siblings, but being the youngest son in a family of eight kids is not fun." Liam was quiet for a moment. "Besides, I hate the city," he said. "I wanted to see what was out west, explore the unknown as you would say."

"Can you tell me more about the Indians?" asked Azariah.

"What is it about them that you would like to know?"

Azariah thought for a moment. He had never even met an Indian and the only information he had on them was what Liam had told him so far. "What are the women like?" he asked nervously.

A huge grin came across Liam's face. "Well, lad," he answered. "You come across some tribes, they will give you a woman."

"As a wife or for something else?"

The Irishman chuckled. "Both," he answered. "Each tribe is different, but in the end, if you show that you are worthy, you will more than likely end up getting yourself a bride for a good price."

Azariah was a little surprised. "They sell their women?"

"I know what you're thinking, lad," said Liam. "And you're wrong, to a point; Indians don't see giving their women to worthy men for a price as slavery."

"How so?" asked Azariah.

"When a warrior wishes to marry a young lady, he must go to her father first," said Liam. "The father would demand that the would-be suitor give him a certain number of horses for his daughter's hand in marriage, like a dowry."

"Oh, I see," said Azariah. "All the tribes do this?"

"Some," answered Liam. "Every tribe is different." Liam paused for a second to refill his pipe and lit it again. "Now, many warriors who go on raiding expeditions against other tribes will sometimes capture women from those tribes."

Azariah was shocked. "What do they do to them?" he asked.

"Most of the time, women from an enemy tribe who are captured are adopted into the tribe of the warrior who captured them," said Liam. "After a certain amount of time, she eventually ends up being the wife of her captor."

"How often does that happen?"

"A lot," answered Liam.

"What if she doesn't want to be adopted or end up being the wife of her captor?" asked Azariah. "She isn't forced against her will, is she?"

"It happens," answered Liam. "But it is rare, at least from what I have seen from living among the Cheyenne."

Azariah was quiet for a moment. Having no experience with women in general, the information that Liam was giving him piqued his curiosity. The closest he ever came to having an experience with a girl was two years ago when he managed to get one of his classmates, Corrine Jackson, to play doctor with him at his house. However, his mother managed to intervene before he got the little lady on the operating table.

"You mention each tribe is different when it comes to courting a lady," he said to Liam. "Just how different?"

"Well, I am no expert," answered Liam. "But I do know that if you wish to court a Cheyenne or an Arapahoe woman, you best keep your hands to yourself until they become your missus."

"Wow!" exclaimed Azariah. "They are that strict?"

Liam nodded. "Cheyenne and Arapahoe are known for their self-control or self-discipline," he said. "Sex before marriage is a huge no-no among them."

Azariah just laughed. "My parents would be interested in them," said Azariah. "They take the Holy Bible literally, especially when it comes to self-discipline."

Now it was Liam's turn to laugh. "I doubt the Good Lord or your parents had the virgin chastity belt in mind."

Azariah was surprised. "Cheyenne women wear chastity belts?!"

"Arapahoe women, too, from what I hear," answered Liam.

"But didn't that go out during the Dark Ages?" asked Azariah. "Don't get me wrong, I am all for chastity and abstinence, but that has to be extreme, even by Indian standards."

Liam chuckled. "I'm sure there are a lot of white over-protective daddies back East who wish we still had the virgin chastity belt." Liam began to yawn and realized it was getting late. "We better get some sleep. We got a long ride tomorrow."

9

The next few days were uneventful as the duo continued to head north. They stuck near the river in case they needed to refill their canteens but did not lower their guards for one second. Then on the fourth day, they saw them.

"We got company," said Liam. "Is your rifle primed?"

Azariah nodded as he saw some Indian riders appear from over the horizon, coming from the north. They didn't look threatening, although they were armed. However, taking a page from his more experienced partner, the youth checked both his rifle and blunderbuss and hoped for the best, but expected the worst.

Azariah quickly realized Liam was smiling as the Indian riders slowly approached them. "I know these men," said Liam. "They are Lakota."

"Are they hostile? The tribe, I mean," asked Azariah.

"They can be, when provoked," answered Liam. "Remember what I told you, you treat them with respect, then they treat you the same way." As the Lakota riders came to a stop in front of the duo, Liam again quickly recognized the leaders and gave a big smile.

"Well, I'll be damned!" he shouted, then started speaking in the Lakota language. "Standing Wolf, my friend, it has been a long time."

"Greetings, Raging Bull," said the tall Lakota warrior known as Standing Wolf. Liam turned to an older Lakota man, who had streaks of gray hair but was well-muscled and had noticeable scars on his chest. There were ten riders in the group, and all but the older man were wearing buckskin shirts and pants. The man was shirtless.

"And how are you, High Cloud?" asked Liam in the Lakota tongue to the old man. High Cloud smiled at Liam and nodded.

"Life has been good to me, Raging Bull," answered High Cloud.

"It must be good to you, old friend," said Liam. "Either you are failing to get any older or there must be a youth potion out here that I don't know about."

Everyone except Azariah laughed. Since he didn't speak any native tongue, he couldn't understand a word Liam and the Lakota men were saying. However, he did relax a bit since it was obvious these men were friends, not enemies.

"So, Standing Wolf, I take it you must be out hunting," Liam remarked.

Standing Wolf nodded, then turned his attention to Azariah. "Who is your new friend?"

"I am sorry. I am being rude," said Liam. "My brothers, this is my friend, Azariah." The men had a hard time pronouncing Azariah's name. High Cloud however managed to say it just as it sounded. "Azariah, allow me to introduce you to Standing Wolf," said Liam. "He is a war chief among the Oglala Lakota and a fine fellow on this side of walking on water." Azariah smiled and extended his hand to Standing Wolf who accepted it. "And this fellow here is High Cloud, a medicine man of their people." Azariah shook High Cloud's hand, who looked at the young man strangely, as if he had met him before.

"It is a pleasure to meet you," said Azariah. Liam translated Azariah's greeting and then introduced him to the rest of the men, most of them young boys, not that much older than himself.

Standing Wolf said something, pointing at Azariah. Liam translated. "Standing Wolf asks how old are you?"

"I am fourteen years old, Chief Standing Wolf," Azariah answered as if he was speaking to someone of authority. When Liam translated, the chief and the medicine man were surprised. High Cloud said something and everyone, including Liam laughed.

"What did he say?" asked Azariah.

"He said fourteen winters? You look like you have seen at least thirty," said Liam.

Azariah just shook his head and smiled. "I have been getting that a lot."

At that point, High Cloud spoke again and signaled everyone to dismount. "He wants to smoke the pipe with us," said Liam. "He said there is much to discuss, and it is about you."

Azariah was shocked. "Me?" Liam nodded. "What about me?" asked Azariah.

Liam just shrugged and said, "Damned if I know, but if they want to smoke the pipe with us, then we should accept their invitation."

Azariah didn't argue. Remembering his mentor's earlier advice about respect, he quickly dismounted and followed Liam and the Lakota warriors as they picked a spot not far from the river. As they sat in a circle, with their legs crossed, each man passed the pipe after smoking it and giving thanks to Wakan Tanka, which meant Great Spirit or Great Mystery in the Lakota tongue. High Cloud never took his eyes off Azariah until the pipe was given to him. He went through the ritual, thanking Wakan Tanka for life and new friends, before passing it to Liam, who repeated the process, before passing it to Azariah. Watching the warriors' example and that of Liam, Azariah gave thanks to Jesus Christ, for new friends, freedom, and life, before smoking the peace pipe and passing it back to Standing Wolf who started the ritual. Liam O'Reilly was impressed with his new pupil, as were Standing Wolf and High Cloud. After the ritual was over, High Cloud spoke at length. Before Liam translated, he had a surprised look on his face as he looked back and forth from the medicine man to Azariah.

"High Cloud says that he has seen you before," Liam finally said to Azariah.

Now it was the young greenhorn's turn to be surprised. "How is that possible?"

Liam asked High Cloud, and the medicine man spoke of a vision that Wakan Tanka gave to him last summer.

In this vision, he was told that he would meet a young *washichu* (Lakota for white man) boy, who walked like a grown man and stood almost as tall as the grizzly bear on his hind legs.

Liam translated this to Azariah, who was both dumbfounded and curious at the same time. "Is Mr. High Cloud sure that he has the right person?" he asked Liam. Liam translated the question.

The medicine man nodded and said more. When he was done, Liam translated, "He said that the Great Spirit has chosen a path for you," said Liam. "He says that you are a man with a good heart and if you decide to walk this path, you will not walk it alone."

Azariah's curiosity piqued. "What does he mean by not walking this path alone?"

Liam translated the question to High Cloud. The medicine man smiled before answering. Liam and some of the warriors, including Standing Wolf, laughed before the Irishman translated the answer. "He said a woman will be with you."

"A woman?" asked Azariah. "What does he mean by a woman? Is he talking about a friend?"

Liam guffawed at the youth's naivety. "Well, that is how getting a wife starts sometimes," he said, chuckling.

Azariah's eyes were wide as saucers. The thought of him getting married as young as he was and having very little experience with the opposite sex was preposterous.

"Tell Mr. High Cloud that he must have the wrong person," said Azariah. "I am too young and too ugly to be any woman's husband."

Liam chuckled before translating Azariah's response. Now it was

High Cloud's turn to laugh. The medicine man spoke as Liam translated.

"In my vision, the Great Spirit told me that you are a man running from his past," he said. "A very painful one."

Both Liam and Azariah were shocked, for the Irishman never told High Cloud or any of the warriors why Azariah came out west with him, and he let Azariah know that he never told them.

"Are you running from your past, He Who Walks Tall?" asked High Cloud. Liam translated the question.

Azariah nodded and then asked, "Who is He Who Walks Tall?"

The medicine man pointed at him and said that is the name he has been given. Azariah couldn't believe what he was hearing. He wasn't even sure if he believed in the religious beliefs of the Lakota, but he was careful not to say anything disrespectful about them; plus, he was wondering if Jesus Christ Himself was putting him on this same path. His head was spinning with questions, especially about the woman who would supposedly walk with him on this chosen path.

"Can you tell me about this woman who will help guide me, if I decide to walk this path that the Great Spirit has chosen?" he asked High Cloud.

Again, the medicine man smiled before responding, saying, "The Great Spirit does not say who she is or what tribe she is," answered High Cloud. "But she will be a red woman from among our allies."

Azariah shook his head in disbelief after Liam translated. He had nothing against High Cloud, in fact, he already found himself liking the man, but he couldn't believe that a God, who the Indians called the Great Spirit, had chosen a path for him. He wasn't even sure if the God he called Jesus Christ and who the Lakota called Wakan Tanka were the same. He didn't want to sound or act disrespectful, but at the same time, he had learned a long time ago from his father that the Lord works in mysterious ways and that sometimes faith itself shouldn't be questioned but accepted.

As if reading the young man's mind, High Cloud spoke. "I know what you are thinking, He Who Walks Tall," he said while Liam translated. "You don't believe or you're not sure if what was said to you today is true or possible." Azariah nodded. High Cloud smiled and lifted his head to the sky as if he were in thought. Strangely enough, Azariah felt that the medicine man reminded him of his father, who would sometimes do the same thing, when in a train of thought. "Faith is never easy to understand when the Great Spirit chooses a path for us," said High Cloud. "But it is real. A man of faith should learn and know to trust when he has been given this gift."

"You sound like my father," said Azariah through Liam's translation. "Among my people, my father is a holy man like yourself."

High Cloud grunted approval. "Then you understand," he said. "Wakan Tanka has chosen a path for you. Trust Him, for it will not be an easy path to take, but you will not walk it alone."

10

A few days later, Liam O'Reilly and Azariah Hancock found themselves at least a few miles from the Wind River Mountains. The
young greenhorn couldn't help but look in sheer awe. Liam chuckled
at the youth, reminding himself of the same reaction he had when he
first came to the mountains so many years ago.

"They're beautiful," said Azariah.

"Like the Garden of Eden, eh?" said Liam.

Azariah nodded. However, at the same time, he couldn't stop
thinking about what High Cloud had said to him, about the path that
was chosen for him. Being a man of faith himself, he was the last
person to question something like that, but he couldn't shake it. Especially the part about having a woman in his life. So far, Azariah was
enjoying his new life as a trapper, despite being a greenhorn.

Before he and Liam left the Oglala hunting party, Chief Standing
Wolf gave the youth an eagle feather as a sign of friendship. Upon the
advice of Liam, Azariah quickly attached the item to his broad-
brimmed hat. In return, he gave the chief and the medicine man,
High Cloud, a cross necklace each. It was a gift from his father who
had a collection of them and would give them out to his congregants.

After the trappers and the hunting party said their goodbyes, Azariah waved goodbye to them and the warriors whooped in response as a sign of respect. Azariah was still thinking about his new name that was given to him by High Cloud. He Who Walks Tall. *What a name,* he thought to himself.

All of a sudden, a gunshot from over a mile away from the north disrupted Azariah's reverie.

"Is that what I think it is?" he asked.

"Aye," answered Liam. More gunshots and whooping noises confirmed that the source was not only human but Indians. "We better take a look, lad," said Liam.

Azariah nodded and checked his guns to see if they were primed and loaded. "Lead the way, Liam." They came over a hill and spotted a village under attack.

Liam took out his spyglass to see which tribe. "They're Arapahoe."

"Didn't you say they are allies to the Cheyenne?" asked Azariah.

"Aye, lad," answered Liam. Liam turned the spyglass to the west to see who was attacking the Arapahoe village. His expression turned red like fire after he put down the spyglass. "The stinking Crow!"

"Another tribe?" asked Azariah.

"Aye," said Liam. "And enemies to the Arapahoe, Cheyenne, and Lakota. They're the bastards who murdered my family!"

"What do we do?" asked Azariah.

Liam took out his Pennsylvania rifle and checked it before answering, "What do you think? I am going down there and offer the Arapahoe a helping hand!"

Azariah was a little shocked but maintained his composure.

"Not by yourself, you're not," he said. "I am coming with you."

"Not your fight, lad," responded the Irishman.

"It is now," argued Azariah. "Friends watch out for each other, and the Arapahoe are your friends, and any friend of yours is a friend of mine."

Liam smiled. "Appreciate the offer, lad," he said. "Stay close and watch your top knot and remember, shoot at those who are shooting at you." After that, the two trappers raced to the Arapahoe village to join in the battle against the Crows.

The Arapahoe village led by White Antelope was under heavy fire from the Crow. Like their allies, the Cheyenne and the Lakota, the Arapahoe were long time enemies of the Crow since time immemorial. Sometimes attacks between the two tribes would be over horses or it perhaps a revenge attack. Either way, frequently, the battles were extremely personal, and this battle was no exception. White Antelope, along with his good friend Two Hawks led a group of their warriors to confront the Crow invaders as they were trying to capture the horses. Little did they know, the Crow brave who was going for the horse herd was a decoy.

Another group of Crow came in from the northeast and went straight for the village. Only a handful of Arapahoe warriors had stayed behind to help defend women, children, and the elderly. They saw the main faction coming toward them and moved to get those who couldn't defend themselves to safety. Among those young warriors who saw the new danger was Two Hawks' son, Howling Wolf.

At sixteen years old, Howling Wolf had already counted at least three coups in his life and has been in battles with the Crow and the Ute. He quickly turned around to get his mother, Clay Basket, and younger sister, Sweet Grass, to safety, before he would join the other defenders to confront the new threat. However, it was too late. The Crow had entered the village and the fighting commenced. Howling Wolf and Wandering Bear, the village medicine man and a close friend of his father, managed to take down three of the enemy with their bows and arrows, before going into hand-to-hand combat. Some of the Crow invaders had rifles, mostly fusees, that they traded with trappers, but most had the traditional bow and arrow and lances, just like the Arapahoe, and both weapons were used indiscriminately. Clay Basket and twelve-year-old Sweet Grass ran to safety with the other women and children. But dread claimed the mother's eyes when she saw three Crow warriors riding towards them from the north. The expression on the invaders' faces was evident. All of sudden, a rifle shot was heard, and the lead Crow's head exploded as he fell backward off his horse. Another shot was heard, coming from behind Clay Basket and Sweet Grass, and a second Crow warrior was shot off his horse. The Arapahoe mother and daughter quickly turned and saw two white men with red hair charging immediately past them and towards the Crow invaders, screaming and whooping at the top of their lungs.

By this time, the battle had almost reached its peak when the newcomers came in. It was clear to the villagers whose side they were on when the older but smaller white man went straight for the last Crow who was approaching Clay Basket and Sweet Grass, but then decided to do a quick U-turn, after seeing two of his comrades sent to the Happy Hunting Grounds. He never made it, as the older redheaded white man caught up to him and quickly buried what appeared to be a Cheyenne tomahawk into his back, causing the Crow to immediately collapse from his horse. The younger but taller redheaded white man stopped for a moment, turned around, and approached Clay Basket and Sweet Grass. He smiled at both of them before his expression changed as he looked past them. The women turned to see two more Crow warriors coming at them. The younger man suddenly lifted his rifle and fired, nearly decapitating one of the warriors and severing the right arm of the other. The younger man then charged at the incapacitated but still alive Crow warrior and immediately took out his pistol and at point-blank range put a bullet in his head.

By this time, the older white man returned and spoke to Clay Basket.

"I am Raging Bull of the Cheyenne," said Liam. "You and your daughter get to safety with the other women and children quickly."

Clay Basket was surprised that the man spoke her tongue, but she did not need to be told twice. She quickly grabbed her daughter, who was still staring at Azariah, and got her to safety. Azariah reloaded his blunderbuss and pistol as he and Liam reentered the village to join the Arapahoe defenders against the Crow. By this time, the invaders saw what the two newcomers did to five of the warriors and assumed that they were part of a larger force. Not caring for those odds, they immediately retreated, but not before a dozen more of their number were cut down by the Arapahoe defenders.

11

With the Crow invaders repelled, the Arapahoe defenders assessed the situation. Some of their warriors were killed, but most of them were wounded, though not badly. Chief White Antelope and Two Hawks returned with the rest of the warriors who fought the decoys. Although some of the brave men lost their lives in defending their village, they were at least grateful to the Man Above that none of the women and children were either hurt or captured by the enemy. Things were not as terrible as they could have been. The chief and the elders were also grateful to the two newcomers, who came in and turned the tide in their favor against their long-hated enemy. White Antelope immediately recognized Liam O'Reilly, better known as Raging Bull. The younger white man he did not know but was amazed and impressed at his height and girth. Raging Bull was talking to Two Hawks' son, Howling Wolf, and the medicine man, Wandering Bear, when they approached the newcomers.

"Greetings, White Antelope," said Liam in the Arapahoe tongue. "It has been a while since we smoked the peace pipe."

"It is good to see you again, Raging Bull," responded White Antelope. "I am grateful for what you and your young friend have done for us today." Two Hawks, who also knew Liam and considered him a friend and ally, shared White Antelope's enthusiasm and praise of the trapper. "Had you not come when you did, Raging Bull, I fear we would have lost many more lives than we did," he said. "We are truly in your debt."

Liam O' Reilly smiled and nodded. He had known these people about as long as he had lived among the Cheyenne and considered them as great friends. "There is no debt between friends and brothers, Two Hawks," he said. "Any friends of the Cheyenne are friends of mine, and I will always gladly call the Arapahoe Nation my brothers."

Before Liam could introduce Azariah, Sweet Grass immediately ran to her father and excitedly spoke so fast to him that Liam could barely keep up. The trapper spoke and understood both the Cheyenne and the Lakota tongue fluently, but he always had a little difficulty catching certain phrases in Arapahoe when the speaker spoke quickly. Azariah was getting nervous, as the girl kept pointing at him while talking to her father. He hoped he hadn't inadvertently done anything that would get him or Liam in any trouble.

Two Hawks and Howling Wolf both looked at Azariah while listening to Sweet Grass, neither smiling nor frowning, which made the young man even more nervous. By the time she was done, her father and brother approached Azariah, who had the look of a terrified fawn about to be a grizzly bear's next appetizer. He quickly turned to Liam, who was smiling a wicked grin as if he just witnessed a cruel joke being played on the greenhorn. Two Hawks stood before the giant teenager. Despite that Azariah was taller than the elder by at least a foot, he sensed that this was a man whose bad side he did not want to get on. He noticed at least eight scalps hanging from Two Hawks' belt and was thinking that his scalp was about to be added. Suddenly, the Arapahoe elder smiled at Azariah then spoke to Liam.

Liam patiently listened and suddenly snickered, before translating what Two Hawks said. "Two Hawks here thanks you for saving the life of his wife and daughter," he said. "His daughter says that other than him and her brother, you are the bravest man that she has ever seen."

Azariah turned beet red as he felt a sense of both being flattered and doomed at the same time. He had never been the type of person who wanted to be the center of attention, due to his shy nature.

"I am honored, sir," said Azariah. "Any friend of Raging Bull is truly a friend of mine." By this time, nearly the entire village had surrounded the newcomers and some of the older folks were surprised at how young Azariah sounded. He looked older than his voice made him out to be, but he sounded like a teenager.

"Who is this brave young man that you have brought among us, Raging Bull?" asked White Antelope. "And how old is he, for he looks like a full-grown man, but his voice says otherwise."

Liam snickered before answering. Gasps went through the crowd as they were astonished. Wandering Bear, who had seen fifty summers, said something to Liam that, even though Azariah didn't understand, he recognized the tone of it, especially after Liam guffawed.

"Wandering Bear here says—" said Liam before being interrupted by Azariah.

"I know, I know. I look like I am at least thirty!"

Liam laughed even louder, before translating back what Azariah said and that caused everyone to laugh.

One of the first lessons that Azariah quickly learned when coming out west was that Indians had a huge sense of humor. The fact that he looked a lot older than he was impressed his newfound friends, especially after how he and Liam helped them repel their enemies, and after they found out that an Oglala Lakota medicine man gave him a name that truly fits him—He Who Walks Tall.

12

After burying their dead and comforting the families of those killed by the Crow, the villagers continued to move to their summer hunting grounds, where the buffalo, elk, deer, and plenty of other game roamed. Liam and Azariah were invited to accompany them. They were the particular guests of Chief White Antelope. Like most of the plains' tribes, the Arapahoe did not have a single chief that ruled an entire tribe or even a village. Anyone could be a chief, but only the bravest, wisest, and most responsible were chosen to be leaders or warriors that the people followed. While men like White Antelope were capable leaders, even they did not have singular authority over their village. Decisions that affected the people were made by a council of elders, along with the chief and sub-chiefs.

This was a thing that Azariah Hancock quickly learned as he and Liam were having dinner with White Antelope and his family. Another thing that the young greenhorn noticed is that Indians, at least among the Arapahoe, take raising children very seriously, including orphans. White Antelope and his wife, Shoots The Enemy Woman, had a total of seven children. Three of those children were adopted. Liam informed Azariah that this was very common among tribes and if one or both parents died or were killed, their children were taken care of by the tribe. Most likely they were adopted by relatives or friends of their parents.

This kind of system of childcare among the tribes was way better than how white orphans are taken care of, Azariah thought to himself.

While they were eating dinner, Azariah realized that he and Liam weren't the only guests at White Antelope's lodge.

Two Hawks and his family had arrived earlier and he, along with White Antelope, was chatting with Liam about his plans and how his Cheyenne relatives were doing. Azariah noticed that Sweet Grass was staring at him and smiling. A little nervous, he smiled back and nodded.

A stifled cough from Sweet Grass' brother, Howling Wolf, got his attention. "My sister is beautiful, isn't she?" asked Howling Wolf using sign language. Azariah, who had been learning sign from Liam recently, was picking up on it and managed to answer the young warrior's question with a yes. Howling Wolf smirked and turned to his father and Liam. He said something in his native tongue, which caused the Irishman to snicker.

"What is it?" asked Azariah.

"It appears that you have an admirer, lad," answered Liam. The youth turned beet red. Then Two Hawks said something to Liam, whose grin grew wider. "Two Hawks here wants to know if you are interested in courting his daughter."

Azariah's eyes nearly bulged out of their sockets in disbelief. "Is he joking?"

"Does he look like he is joking, lad?" asked Liam sarcastically.

"But... but I don't know anything about women," said Azariah. "Especially about courting one."

"Then you're S-O-L on that one, lad," laughed Liam. "But, hey, like me poppa always said, experience is the best teacher."

Azariah felt like he was between a rock and a hard place. He looked at Sweet Grass, and for the first time, he saw that she was very beautiful. More beautiful than any woman he had ever seen. Even though she was probably not that much younger than him, most folks would consider her still a child. He, as well.

"Well, do you want to court the pretty lass or not?" asked Liam.

Azariah nodded and then asked, "How does one go about courting an Arapahoe lady?"

"It's simple," said Liam. "You both go walking under a blanket or buffalo robe through the village and talk to each other."

"Just like that?"

"Aye, lad."

Azariah thought for a moment before asking some more questions. "Is there anything else I need to know?"

"You know how to play the flute?" asked Liam. Azariah shook his head. "Some suitors play the flute when courting a lady," said Liam.

Azariah swallowed a bit and then sighed. "Kindly tell Mr. Two Hawks that I would be honored to court his daughter."

Liam translated to Two Hawks. Two Hawks said something to his daughter and then asked a question to Azariah that Liam translated. "He asks how about now?"

Azariah almost choked. "Right now?" he asked.

"Sure," said Liam.

Azariah started to sweat. Sweet Grass immediately got her buffalo robe and approached the young greenhorn.

"What do I do?" asked Azariah.

"You go out first and she follows you, then you put the buffalo robe over both of you," answered Liam.

Azariah got up and nervously bowed to Two Hawks and Chief White Antelope, before heading out of the tent with Sweet Grass. The boy was as nervous as a condemned prisoner being escorted to the gallows. Just as soon as he and Sweet Grass were outside the teepee, they both could hear laughter from all the men inside. Azariah suspected that his mentor led in that.

13

It was getting dark, but not dark enough for Azariah to see the whites of Sweet Grass' eyes. *What on Earth am I doing?* he asked himself. The young greenhorn was as nervous as an ex-prostitute entering her first church service. Here he was in the middle of an Arapaho village, walking hand in hand with the only daughter of one of the head village elders under a buffalo robe, and he was sweating like a pig. Not wanting to look or act like the village idiot, Azariah decided to break the ice and spoke with Sweet Grass, completely forgetting that she knew no English whatsoever.

"It is such a beautiful night, don't you think?" he asked her.

Sweet Grass just stared at him, not understanding. Completely embarrassed, Azariah corrected his error and repeated the question using sign language. The girl smiled and nodded. With those perfectly white and even teeth, the young man's knees almost went out from under him, before he corrected himself.

They continued to walk through the village under the buffalo robe until they bumped into two young men that Sweet Grass immediately recognized. Otter Tail and Beaver both were around Azariah's age and had been close friends of Howling Wolf.

"Greetings, He Who Walks Tall," said Beaver in English. Azariah was amazed and asked the young man where he learned the white man's tongue. Turns out that his aunt was happily married to a trapper and they lived in another village not far from White Antelope's village. He often spent time with his aunt, her husband, and their children and that husband taught him the white man's tongue.

"I am impressed," said Azariah. "Maybe soon, you, Raging Bull and Sweet Grass can teach me how to speak Arapaho."

Beaver laughed before translating what was said to Otter Tail and Sweet Grass. The girl giggled when Otter Tail responded. "He says if you continue to court Howling Wolf's sister, you might learn it a lot sooner than you think," translated Beaver.

Azariah was about to ask Beaver what Otter Tail meant by that, but Sweet Grass got his attention by pulling on his sleeve and pointing to the lake, indicating that she wanted to go there for some privacy. Azariah nodded and said his goodbyes to his two new Arapaho friends before walking with Sweet Grass to the lake. They sat down by the edge of the lake on a stone, staring up at the stars for a moment before she got his attention again.

"How did you get the name He Who Walks Tall," she asked in sign language.

Azariah managed to finally get over his shyness and through his limited knowledge of the universal Indian sign language, explained to Sweet Grass about his meeting with the Oglala Lakota medicine man, High Cloud, and his vision about him given by Wankan Tanka. He told how he couldn't believe it at first because his own religious beliefs were not the same as the Lakota's, but being the son of a white medicine man, he was taught that sometimes faith shouldn't be questioned but accepted.

"Your father is a medicine man?" asked Sweet Grass with a look of surprise.

Azariah smiled and shrugged. "Yes and no," he answered in sign. "Among us whites, holy men are not called medicine men. We don't even call them holy, although we hold them to higher standards."

"What do you call them?"

"I don't think there is a word for them in your tongue." Azariah paused for a moment and then said, "Preachers. That is what we call them." Sweet Grass repeated the word over and over again before she got it right, but with a more guttural sound to it. Then through sign, she asked Azariah what his real name is.

"Azariah Hancock."

"Azariawww," she repeated. "Azariawww Hand Cock!"

Azariah snickered. He found himself liking this pretty, obviously intelligent Arapaho maiden. As she was saying his full name over and over again, he thought to himself, *What would my parents think? Courting an Indian maiden, a heathen to be exact.* He remembered his father telling him that we are all God's children, black, white, red, Christian and heathen alike, but did he have in mind his only son courting a heathen Indian girl?

Azariah was brought out of his reverie when he felt Sweet Grass' hand touch his hair. She was gently pulling it, while she was smiling at him.

"What is it?" he asked in sign.

"I like your hair," she answered. "I have never seen such red hair before."

Suddenly Azariah's blood began to rise, but his shyness and nervousness returned as well, so he felt compelled to ask, "Have you ever kissed a man before?" Sweet Grass giggled and slowly shook her head. "I have never kissed a woman," said Azariah. "May I kiss you?"

Sweet Grass nodded as Azariah gently lifted her chin with his huge hand and kissed her. It was only for a moment, but for both of them, it felt like a young bear getting its first taste of honey and being immediately hooked. Azariah enjoyed it but was concerned whether Sweet Grass felt the same. She confirmed it when she wrapped her arms around his neck and gave him another kiss. This time it lasted a hell of a lot longer than the first.

14

Azariah and Liam stayed with the Arapahos for a week. During that time, Azariah spent what little free time he had courting Sweet Grass, under the watchful eye of her father Two Hawks. Apparently, since their first kiss, the young maiden had been walking around with a huge grin on her face as if she were on cloud nine. Azariah for his part would help around the village and learn the Arapaho language as much as he could, so he could converse with Sweet Grass. About two nights after their first kiss, they were by the lake enjoying a second kiss only to be caught by Two Hawks and Wandering Bear, the medicine man. Since then, Azariah was only allowed to court Sweet Grass near her parents' lodge, which was okay with him; except her brother, Howling Wolf, and Liam were both pains in his ass, continually teasing him, which drove the young lovesick green-horn up the wall.

By the following week, Liam was eager to be on the move, wanting to see his Cheyenne relatives and in-laws. The very day they were to depart, Sweet Grass approached Azariah with a gift. It was a puppy, from one of the village dogs. Azariah was pleased with this gift and promised Sweet Grass, come hell or high-water, he would return.

"And I will make sure he keeps that promise," said Liam with a grin.

Suddenly, Azariah removed a crucifix from his neck. "My mother gave me this," he said as he gave it to Sweet Grass. "I would be honored if you wear it." Sweet Grass turned to her father as if asking for permission. Two Hawks nodded and Azariah had her turn around as he put the necklace around her neck.

"Will you return?" asked Sweet Grass.

"Yes, I will."

She then kissed him fully on the lips, shocking her parents.

Public displays of affection between courting couples were considered taboo among the tribes, and the Arapaho were no exception. Two Hawks and Clay Basket liked Azariah but felt that the giant white boy had somehow put a spell on their only daughter, which worried them. However, Howling Wolf, Wandering Bear, Otter Tail, and Beaver felt that it was Sweet Grass who may have put a spell on him. Of course, no one would dare say that to Two Hawks to his face.

"Time to get a move on, Romeo," said Liam.

Azariah reluctantly released his embrace of Sweet Grass, took the puppy, tucked it in his coat, and hopped on his horse. As they rode out of the village of White Antelope, Azariah paused for a moment, turned his horse around, and raised his hat to the villagers as he waved goodbye. The villagers responded with cheers and whoops. Liam just sat there on his horse, grinning as usual.

"What are you smiling about?" asked Azariah.

"You truly have the makings of a mountaineer," answered the Irishman.

Azariah smiled at the praise, then looked at the small puppy, who was licking his face. It was a male and Azariah automatically fell in love with it. Then his thoughts quickly turned to Sweet Grass.

As if reading his young protégé's thoughts, Liam spoke. "Don't worry, lad. You will see her again."

"How can you be so sure?"

"Simple. The Arapahos and the Cheyennes are not only close allies, their territories are not that far from each other."

"Oh," said Azariah.

Liam looked at the dog. "What you going to name him?"

"I am going to name him Gideon," answered Azariah.

"Good name," said Liam.

The duo along with their new pet headed to the north towards Cheyenne country.

15

A couple of weeks later, the duo and their new pet, Gideon, arrived at the Cheyenne village of Black Cloud, near the Tongue River. Black Cloud was the head chief and leader in this village and a long-time friend of Liam. He and the Irishman were the same age and had been on many hunts and battles together. As he watched his friend arrive with a stranger, who was a giant, he felt the presence of another friend stand beside him. It was none other than He Dog, Liam's father-in-law. He Dog was much older than both Black Cloud and Liam, which made him an elder on the council. Black Cloud often went to him for advice concerning the village, family, and even the council itself. Black Cloud may have been the leader and head chief, but he quickly and humbly recognized that he did not have sole authority over the village or the warriors who protected the village. However, people followed him, because even as young as he was, he was a proven leader in the eyes of the people and those in the council. He Dog was one of two of his closest supporters and allies when he was made chief. The other was Liam, who despite not being born a Cheyenne, as an adopted Cheyenne he sat on the council and, like

Black Cloud, had proven himself a loyal and brave warrior who put the people's interests over his own.

To see the man now called Raging Bull return, after being gone many moons, was a reason to celebrate. He Dog knew that Liam loved his daughter very much and her loss and the loss of their baby at the hands of the Crow nearly destroyed him, despite avenging their deaths. He Dog had long worried over his son-in-law's state of mind, for Liam had not remarried nor even thought about seeking another woman. However, the elder respected Liam's space and privacy and didn't push. He planned to talk to him about it later, but now wasn't the time. He was happy to see him again and wanted to meet this new stranger he brought.

Liam and the stranger stopped their horses in front of He Dog and Black Cloud. "Greetings, Black Cloud," said Liam in the Cheyenne tongue.

"Welcome home, Raging Bull," responded Black Cloud. "It has been many moons."

"Too long if you ask me, my brother," said Liam.

The Irishman paused and then turned to He Dog. He gave his father-in-law a huge hug, rekindling the bond between them.

"Welcome home, my son," said He Dog. "It is good to see that Maheo has protected you."

"That and more, Father," said Liam. Liam quickly noticed the approach of his brother-in-law, Spotted Eagle, his wife, Red Sun, and their three sons, Sparrow, Badger, and Black Wolf. The Irishman felt like he had truly returned home to family.

"It is good to see you again, brother," said Spotted Eagle.

"Likewise, Spotted Eagle," responded Liam. "Maheo shines on you and your loved ones, I see."

"We have much to be thankful for," responded Spotted Eagle. "I scarcely know where to begin." By this time, two more of He Dog's sons, Pawnee Killer and Thunder Cloud, arrived, along with their mother, Song Bird, and their sister, Red Willow, and her husband, Running Fox. By the time they came to greet Liam and his friend and welcome them home, the whole village had surrounded them. Some of the children were asking Liam a dozen questions all at once before their grandparents gently silenced them and allowed the Irishman to introduce his new friend.

"Friends and family," said Liam, "allow me to introduce to you my young friend, He Who Walks Tall."

Azariah smiled and waved at everyone as Liam translated his introduction to the village.

Chief Black Cloud looked approvingly at the young man and quickly welcomed him. "Any friend of Raging Bull is a friend of mine and my people," he said in English. Azariah was amazed at how well the Cheyenne chief spoke his tongue.

"Thank you," he said. "Did Liam, excuse me, Raging Bull teach you the white man's tongue?"

Black Cloud smiled and nodded. "How did you get the name He Who Walks Tall?"

Azariah looked at Liam.

"Don't look at me, lad. It's to you he asked the question."

The youth smiled and said, "A Lakota medicine man named High Cloud gave me this name."

Black Cloud translated to the rest of the family and village. Many of the elders and warriors nodded in approval and were impressed at the name given to Azariah but were still surprised at his voice. He looked like a full-grown man and more but sounded like a young boy. He Dog, who also spoke English, but only spoke with white men he knew and trusted like Liam, asked Azariah his age. The young man smiled as he saw an impish grin on Liam's face before he answered He Dog's question.

"I have seen fourteen winters."

Both He Dog and Black Cloud were amazed and amused at the same time and showed it before the elder translated to the people, who were likewise amazed that one so young could be so big and tall.

"Fourteen winters!" exclaimed Pawnee Killer in Cheyenne. "You looked like you have seen at least thirty!"

Everyone laughed, including Azariah. Even though he didn't speak the Cheyenne tongue yet, he knew the tone and didn't need to hear the translation. Pawnee Killer was the second eldest of He Dog and Song Bird's five children, and he was also a known prankster. However, he was also considered one of the most underrated warriors as far as bravery went among the village and along with his eldest brother, Spotted Eagle, was a member of the Dog Soldiers.

Liam quickly introduced He Dog, Song Bird, and the rest of his in-laws to Azariah who greeted them with his usual humility and respect. Towards Song Bird, Red Sun, and the wives of Spotted Eagle, Pawnee Killer, and Thunder Cloud, he gave a bow while doffing his hat. The women thought this humorous, even though Liam had explained to them that is how a white gentleman greets a lady. Thunder Cloud and Running Fox noticed the dog standing next to Azariah and assumed it was a gift for dinner.

Among many of the plains tribes, including the Cheyenne and Arapahoe, a dog was considered a delicacy. It was also Thunder Cloud and Running Fox's favorite dish and greatly appreciated every time their wives cooked it for dinner. Liam O'Reilly knew this and quickly informed them that Gideon belonged to He Who Walks Tall and was not food, but a pet. Thunder Cloud just shook his head and laughed, while Running Fox had a dumbfounded look on his face.

"This dog is your pet?" asked Running Fox to Azariah. The boy nodded after the question was translated by He Dog. "You white men are strange indeed."

"Why would you say that?" asked Azariah, hurt.

"Because why keep an animal as a pet and give it a name as if it is family when one day you might have to eat it?" answered Running Fox.

Azariah thought for a moment and pondered the warrior's statement. It made a lot of sense, but Gideon was more than just a pet and a friend to him. "My dog was a gift given to me by a special woman." Liam translated the statement and noticed that there were smirks on some of the men's faces, including He Dog, Black Cloud, Spotted Eagle and even Running Fox.

"Ah, she must be very special to give you such a gift that you are willing to treat it more like family than food," said Running Fox.

Azariah turned beet red.

Everyone immediately knew that the warrior was spot on. "We should discuss this later," said He Dog. "Raging Bull is home, and he has brought a new friend of the people. You are both welcome in my lodge."

"Thank you, Father," said Liam. "I am looking forward to mother Song Bird's cooking again." Everyone laughed, including Song Bird, who by her admission was not the greatest cook among Cheyenne women. Her husband often teased her about it, and Liam always said she was too modest, however, her son-in-law was a bad flatterer like her husband.

"Tell He Who Walks Tall that because he is a guest, I will cook a special dish for him," said Song Bird. He Dog translated to Azariah, who then had anticipation on his face.

"I am honored, ma'am," he said. "What special dish will you be serving?" Song Bird pointed to Gideon, and Azariah's expression turned to a look of horror. "No, please, not my dog!"

Everyone in the village busted out laughing at Song Bird's practical joke on the giant youth.

16

The following weeks were busy for the entire village of Black Cloud. It was now the middle of July, and the buffalo had returned. Liam and Azariah had joined He Dog, Spotted Eagle, Pawnee Killer, and Thunder Cloud, along with some of the younger boys, who weren't yet warriors but old enough to go on a hunt, to ride out to the herd and bring in some meat. The buffalo herd was at least three miles from the village and, as usual, far from being a small one. Once the hunters came upon them, Azariah still couldn't help but be amazed at how many buffalo there were. At least in this herd, there looked to be enough to feed the entire Cheyenne Nation, if not every tribe in the northern Rockies. At least that is what Azariah thought. Liam had explained earlier the night before to Azariah how the buffalo would be hunted. They would be going on a surround, in which the hunters would cause a stampede and run down the shaggy beasts. Sometimes hunters would use both the lances or bows and arrows while riding from the backs of their horses to bring down a beast.

"Sounds pretty dangerous," said Azariah.

Liam smiled. "It is dangerous, lad."

"Then why hunt that way?" asked Azariah. "Wouldn't it be easier and safer if they just used a bow and arrow from a safe distance and took the buffalo down that way?"

"Where's the bloody fun in that?" laughed the Irishman. "Live out here long enough and you will learn that no way of hunting a dangerous animal is safe." Liam paused for a moment, before continuing, "Sometimes you just have to live for the moment, and that is why a lot of Indians and trappers alike go on a buffalo surround. It's the excitement of the hunt that gets the blood running."

Azariah thought for a moment, then smiled. "I see your point."

As they approached the herd, Azariah thought about Sweet Grass. He prayed he wouldn't get hurt or worse, get killed on this hunt. He wanted to see her again. At that moment he removed the thought from his mind and focused on the task at hand when He Dog whooped a loud yell, which signaled the rest of the hunting party to move.

The whooping and the hollering had the intended effect as the herd moved in the direction the hunters wanted them to go. Liam, on his white Appaloosa stallion, was riding at top speed following Spotted Eagle, who had already loosed five arrows into a buffalo cow. The beast immediately went down at full speed after the fifth arrow hit a vital organ. Liam had shot a bull with his Pennsylvania rifle, hitting the heart, which caused its demise, before he reloaded almost as quickly as his brother-in-law was firing arrows. Azariah, along with Running Fox and Pawnee Killer, were right behind them. The youth managed to hit a cow with his rifle, but the beast didn't go down. He missed an organ. Reloading while in the middle of riding his black stallion at full speed was a difficult feat, but he managed to do so and catch up to the wounded animal, firing a second shot, this time hitting the heart. The greenhorn whooped like a full-blooded Cheyenne in rejoicing. Pawnee Killer, who had just taken down a bull, quickly rode up to Azariah and patted him on the back, knowing that this was the first time he had hunted buffalo during a surround. Then suddenly a look of horror came to the faces of both men when a wounded and enraged bull knocked twelve-year-old Sparrow off his horse.

Sparrow's horse got the worst of it as the buffalo's horns ripped open its belly. Sparrow had the wind knocked out of him as he landed on his side. Fortunately, nothing was broken. He was back on his feet, just as the enraged bull turned his attention to him. Spotted Eagle was too far away to reach his son in time. All he could do was yell; however, Pawnee Killer and Azariah were closer. As the boy ran for his life, his uncle unleashed arrow after arrow into the bull, which was closing in on him. Filled with adrenaline and testosterone and rage, the arrows appeared to have little effect on the seven-foot, nearly twelve-hundred-pound beast that was less than a hair's breadth from ramming its deadly horns into the boy. Suddenly a loud bang sounded, and the buffalo bull immediately fell a few feet from Sparrow.

The boy was quivering as the beast lay dead at his feet. He didn't even notice his father, uncles, grandfather, along with Liam approaching. "Are you all right?" asked a concerned Spotted Eagle as he jumped off his horse and hugged his son. He Dog and the others immediately dismounted and ran lances through the beast just to make sure it was dead.

"I am... I am okay, Father," said Sparrow. "At least, I think I am."

"Where did that shot come from?" asked Liam as he examined the dead bull and noticed a huge hole near the heart.

"You didn't shoot the beast, Raging Bull?" asked He Dog. Liam shook his head.

"It couldn't have been Raging Bull," said Spotted Eagle. "He was with me, and we were both too far to even get into range to save my son."

Just then, Azariah rode up with his blunderbuss still smoking.

"It was He Who Walks Tall that saved your son, my brother," said Pawnee Killer. "When my arrows couldn't slow down the beast, I saw him aim his strange rifle at it."

"So that's where the loud bang came from," laughed Liam. "I forgot you had a blunderbuss with you, lad!!"

Just as soon as Azariah dismounted, Spotted Eagle approached him and put his hands on the boy's shoulders. "I am forever in your debt."

"I was just glad I was able to help," said Azariah. "But I didn't do this alone. Pawnee Killer must have unleashed a dozen arrows into that monster."

Pawnee Killer was flattered and humbled by the youth's praise but refused to take credit for saving the life of his nephew. "It was your thunder stick that killed the bull and saved Sparrow's life, He Who Walks Tall."

Liam and He Dog, along with others, patted Azariah on the back, while Sparrow walked up and thanked him for saving his life. Azariah just smiled and nodded. Not one to enjoy attention, good or bad, Azariah remained tight-lipped. This did not go unnoticed, for Liam and He Dog tried to let him know what he had done was no small thing and he should be proud. Thunder Cloud then approached the buffalo, cut it open, and took out its heart. He offered the severed organ to Azariah, who at first was a little hesitant, but Liam encouraged him to accept it and take a bite. The greenhorn did and chewed the bloody meat and even savored it.

"It's good," he said.

Everyone cheered and whooped as Azariah then handed the buffalo heart to Sparrow, who accepted and took a bite.

Liam just smiled at his protégé and said, "Lad, you truly have the makings to be a mountaineer."

17

After the hunt, a great feast was held in Azariah's honor. Hunting a herd of buffalo by way of a surround was the most dangerous method of hunting in the West, but when it came to hunting these huge shaggy beasts, there was no truly safe method. Buffalo, like the equally dangerous and ferocious grizzly bear, were notoriously hard to kill, whether by bows and arrows, lances, or firearms. They were created with a built-in body armor of fat, and a thick layer of skin. Standing between six to seven feet at the shoulder on all fours and weighing up to at least fifteen hundred pounds, the American Buffalo or Bison is a formidable animal. Even the feared grizzly bear and packs of wolves, which are its two main predators, other than man, approach it with a sense of caution. Many hunters, both white and red alike, have been killed by the giant shaggy beasts, either gored to death, or worse, stampeded by an entire herd. The buffalo was truly an animal not to be underestimated.

The fact that no one was killed on this hunt was considered a true miracle and a blessing from Maheo Himself, according to the village of Black Cloud. Azariah felt that saving Sparrow's life was nothing, since he would've done it for anyone, or Sparrow would've done the same thing for him; however, to Sparrow's family and the Cheyenne boy, it was a big deal. Azariah, who was only two years older than Sparrow, felt he found himself a new friend. That, at least, didn't bother him at all. Liam was more like a big brother to Azariah than a close friend, and since the greenhorn didn't have any brothers of his own back in Maryland, not to mention many friends, it wasn't long before he and Sparrow started hanging out together.

During the next couple of days, Azariah through sign language was learning the Cheyenne tongue from Sparrow and his brothers—Badger, who was nine, and Black Wolf, who was seven. In return, he was teaching them English and also how to use a rifle and a blunderbuss. When they weren't learning each other's languages, the boys would go fishing and horse racing around the village. The boys also enjoyed watching Azariah train Gideon to do tricks as well as teaching the pup lessons on how to obey and follow commands.

During the rest of the summer, Azariah was starting to miss the Arapahos, Sweet Grass in particular. He mentioned as much to Liam and asked when they would return to the village of White Antelope. Liam assured his young friend that they would return, but it would be a while. "We have to help the village head to their winter camp," he said. "Fall will be coming soon, and after we're done with that, we still have to head to my cabin in the Beartooth Mountains."

"How long will that take?" asked Azariah.

"Don't know, lad," said Liam. "Trapping season starts around the same time the village reaches their winter camp, and that is when your lessons start."

Azariah looked depressed. He missed Sweet Grass, and he also missed his friends from her village, Beaver and Otter Tail. He liked hanging out with Sparrow and also learning the Cheyenne language and their culture as well. He felt right at home, just like he did among the Arapahos. But for some reason, it didn't feel the same, for he wanted Sweet Grass. He couldn't stop thinking about her, and the pup, Gideon, often reminded him of her, since she was the one who gave him to Azariah as a gift.

Azariah quickly noticed his friend smirking. "What are you smiling about?"

"I know you miss your little Arapahoe Juliet."

"Shut up!"

The Irishman laughed and patted the greenhorn on his back. "Relax, lad," he said. "You will see her again soon. Remember the Arapahos and the Cheyenne are close allies and don't live that far from each other."

"How far is your cabin?" asked Azariah. "You said it was somewhere in the Beartooth Mountains."

"About a couple of days' ride northwest from here."

Azariah huffed under his breath. He feared he might not see Sweet Grass again until the end of the year and it was almost August already. "I don't know if I could wait until trapping season starts, Liam."

"Good things come to those who wait, lad," said the Irishman. "Besides, if it is love, she will wait for you."

Azariah's spirits lifted a bit and he smiled at his mentor. "Okay. Whatever you think is best."

At that moment, Spotted Eagle approached with three fine horses. He was followed by Sparrow and He Dog. "He Who Walks Tall, I wish to give you these horses as a token of my thanks," said Spotted Eagle in Cheyenne.

Azariah had picked up much of the language as fast as he picked up the Arapahoe tongue. "Thank you, Spotted Eagle, but I have done nothing to deserve such gifts."

"You saved my eldest son's life," responded Spotted Eagle. "If that is not worthy of a gift, I don't know what is."

Azariah knew enough that to not accept would mean an insult, so he didn't reject the presents. "I accept these gifts with great joy," he said. "But your son's friendship, as well as the friendship of the people, is truly a gift beyond measure." The warrior and his father were impressed and touched, and they let the youth know it.

"I trust that these three horses will make a great bride price," said He Dog.

Azariah was dumbfounded. "A bride price, for who?"

The Cheyenne elder gave an impish grin. "For this Arapahoe girl you like so much that Raging Bull keeps talking about."

Azariah turned beet red as he chased his mentor all over the village. "Liam, you bigmouth Irish son of a bitch!"

18

It was October, and the village of Black Cloud had moved to their winter camp south of what is now Denver, Colorado. During the summer, they had stocked up on meat, drying it on racks to save for times such as this. Azariah and Liam headed to the Beartooth Mountains at the beginning of September to prepare for the fall trapping season. Azariah, as usual, was an adept student of the trade. Checking his traps three times a day, he caught at least fifty beaver his first week, a feat that impressed Liam. During their free time, they would stretch out their pelts so they would be sleek and catch a good price once they traveled back to St. Louis after the spring trapping season.

Under the Irishman's tutelage, Azariah also became an adept hunter, bringing back elk, moose, and even bighorn sheep, which was Liam's favorite. After making pemmican from their hunts, the duo cached their beaver plews, which now numbered one hundred and twenty, near the cabin and traveled out of the Beartooth Mountains down to the Yellowstone region to look for new trapping grounds. Gideon was getting big and became a dutiful companion to both his master and his mentor. He quickly learned how to be obedient and learned some hunting tricks that came in handy every time Azariah went out hunting by himself. The animal also became an excellent watchdog, keeping a lookout for enemies of both the four- and two-legged variety. From the Beartooth Mountains to the Yellowstone River were considered Crow country, and the Crow, as Azariah knew, had an ongoing feud with Liam and the Cheyenne, as well as the Arapaho.

But they weren't the only enemy tribe the duo had to be on the lookout for. Where they were traveling was also known to be the favorite invading spot of the dreaded members of the Blackfoot Confederacy, whose territory was farther north towards Canada in the area now known as Glacier National Park. Called Bug's Boys by the trappers, the Blackfeet were known as the Lords of the Northern Plains, and they were considered enemies of nearly every other tribe of the Northern Plains, such as the Flathead, Nez Perce, Shoshone, Lakota, Cheyenne, Arapaho, Cree, Chippewa, Assiniboine, and the Crow. They were allies of the Atsina Tribe, who the trappers called Gros Ventre, but they were not related. The Blackfoot Confederacy consisted of three clans: Siksika (Blackfoot Proper), Pikuni (Piegan), and Kainah (Blood). Even though their territory was north of the Beartooth Mountains, they traveled wherever they pleased.

The Blackfeet, along with their Atsina allies, went where the buffalo went and had no problem invading other tribes' territories. Their main and biggest tribal enemy was the Crow. But they hated the trappers more than they hated any other enemy they had ever had. Liam mentioned this much to Azariah as they traveled to the Yellowstone.

"Why don't the Blackfeet like us?" asked Azariah.

"You ever heard of Meriwether Lewis, lad?" responded Liam.

"From the Lewis and Clark Expedition?"

"The same."

"What does he have to do with them?" asked Azariah.

"John Colter told me that on their way back from the West, they camped near the Two Medicine River region in Blackfoot country," said Liam. "One night, some teenage Piegan boys wanted to make a name for themselves so they tried to steal Meriwether Lewis' horse, but that didn't end so well." Azariah wasn't sure he liked where this was heading. "One of the men from the expedition, George Drouillard was his name, he was half-Shawnee Indian and half-French, was fighting with one of those boys because he was trying to steal his rifle," said Liam. "In the end, Meriwether Lewis ended up shooting not one but two of those teenagers in the back."

"That's terrible," said Azariah. "From what you have told me, Indians don't consider it stealing. If you are unable to look after your belongings, didn't you say it was like a game to them?"

"Aye, lad," answered Liam. "But from what John Colter told me, old Captain Lewis wasn't right in the head and felt that shooting two unarmed Blackfoot teenagers in the back was the solution to keep them from stealing."

"So the Blackfeet have held a grudge against all white men, because of that?"

"Aye, lad," answered Liam. "But I believe it goes deeper than that, though."

"How so?"

"Well, the Blackfeet are very war-like, just like any other tribe," said Liam. "Don't get me wrong. I believe they are fighting to protect what is theirs, just like any other tribe in these parts. That is why I don't go trapping in their country, for any reason."

"You know trappers who have?" asked Azariah.

"Aye," answered Liam. "Me good friend John Colter, and that nearly cost him his life twice, and George Drouillard, who wasn't as lucky as John." Azariah sensed some sadness coming from his mentor and friend. "As far as them hating and holding a grudge against all white men, I wouldn't go that far," said Liam. "I know trappers that have worked for the damned Hudson Bay Company have managed to trade with them."

"I remember you telling me about them," said Azariah. "Goes

with you saying that trappers have more to fear from each other than they do from Indians."

"Exactly, lad," said Liam with a grin.

They managed to reach the Yellowstone River and set up camp. While Azariah was getting the fire started and preparing coffee, Liam searched the perimeter around the river and found many beaver lodges. Once he was satisfied, he returned to camp just in time, as the coffee was ready and Azariah was cooking some biscuits and beans along with some jerked elk meat from their stores.

"Find any beaver lodges?" asked the youth as he handed a cup of coffee to the Irishman.

"Plenty, lad," answered Liam. "We start setting our traps in the morning." At that moment, Gideon was growling at the opposite side of camp and the horses that were staked out were whinnying frantically. Azariah and Liam quickly grabbed their rifles as they immediately saw the cause for the commotion approaching out of the darkness. A huge male grizzly bear crawled into the firelight, smelling the food that Azariah had cooked, wanting to investigate.

"Tell your dog to be silent and don't move a muscle, lad," cautioned Liam.

Azariah knew better than to question his mentor, especially at a time such as this. Grizzly bears were extremely dangerous and notoriously hard to kill, especially if they were in a killing mood. This beast was larger than most Liam had ever seen. On average, a male grizzly stood at six feet to the shoulder while on all fours, but this one stood at nearly nine feet to the shoulder on all fours and probably weighed about as much as an adult buffalo.

"He is probably just investigating," whispered Liam. "They have very poor eyesight, but a terrific sense of smell."

"Is that supposed to make me feel better?" asked Azariah, not taking his eyes off the beast.

The Irishman slowly shook his head. Azariah had quietly told Gideon to stand still and be silent, but the dog, sensing danger and feeling bravado, not only growled but charged at the huge bruin.

"Dammit!" shouted Liam.

The grizzly immediately stood on his hind legs as the dog charged to attack. Gideon leaped up at the beast, but in mid-leap, the grizzly swiped the dog with his huge right paw as if it were a pesky little insect. Gideon yelped as he was knocked ten feet into a tree. Seeing his pet in trouble, Azariah immediately picked up his Pennsylvania rifle, aimed, and fired into the chest of Old Ephraim, as the trappers called the grizzly bear. The bullet found its mark, but instead of downing the giant beast, it only pissed him off to the tenth degree. The grizzly roared as he returned to all fours and charged.

"Scatter!" shouted Liam as he fired his rifle at the beast, its bullet finding its mark, hitting the animal below the shoulder.

Azariah ran to get his blunderbuss and managed to turn around just in time to see Old Ephraim coming at him.

"Get your ass up a tree, Azariah!" shouted Liam as he was quickly reloading his rifle and trying to chase the grizzly to get him away from his young friend. But Azariah was momentarily paralyzed with fear. The grizzly stood on his hind legs and was about to tear the young trapper apart. However, in that split second, Azariah raised his loaded blunderbuss and fired into the chest of the beast. Before he knew it, everything went black.

19

Meanwhile, back at the foot of the Wind River Mountain range, the Arapahoe village of White Antelope had just finished setting up for winter. Early that morning, Sweet Grass had suddenly awakened in a cold sweat. Ever since meeting the giant white boy she called Azari-aww, she couldn't stop thinking about him. She would have dreams of them together as husband and wife, raising a whole passel of children. She would often tell her mother, Clay Basket, and the medicine man, Wandering Bear, about these dreams. Clay Basket would pass it off as the childish fantasy of a young girl, but Wandering Bear thought otherwise. Like most of the people in the village, he liked Azariah, or He Who Walks Tall as he was known to the tribes. There was something about the young man that showed he was destined to walk a certain path chosen by the Man Above and that Sweet Grass was meant to be by his side, not just as a wife and mother to his children, but also as someone to guide him on that path.

Wandering Bear remembered what Liam O'Reilly told him about how a Lakota medicine man gave Azariah the name He Who Walks Tall, which gave the Arapahoe medicine man lots of food for thought.

He accepted that maybe that giant white youth was chosen by the Great Spirit to walk a certain path in his life and that Sweet Grass was chosen to be his wife. However, he wouldn't dare tell Two Hawks or Clay Basket that. Not to their faces, at least. Sweet Grass' parents had nothing against Azariah, for he was not just a friend of Raging Bull but a proven, honorable man in his own right. That still didn't mean they were too excited about their only daughter being married to a white man.

Two Hawks himself expressed concerns about this to Sweet Grass, but Howling Wolf would often try to convince his father that Sweet Grass could do much worse than taking Azariah for a mate. That is, if she would ever see him again, which was the cause of her current dilemma as she continued to wipe the cold sweat from her brow.

"Bad dream?" asked Clay Basket.

Sweet Grass nodded to her mother as she slowly got out from under the buffalo robes and managed to get dressed. The sun hadn't yet risen, but it was not unusual to find Clay Basket awake and getting the morning meal ready at this time, for she had always been a light sleeper. She sensed that something was bothering her daughter.

"You were thinking about him again?"

"How did you know?" asked Sweet Grass.

"I'm your mother. I always know these things."

Sweet Grass left the lodge to go down to the lake to wash herself up. The weather was colder than most mornings in the middle of autumn, but it wasn't freezing yet. She quickly returned to help her mother get things ready for breakfast, but her father and brother were still asleep.

"Your father and I have been meaning to talk to you about He Who Walks Tall," said Clay Basket. Sweet Grass knew where this was going. "He is a good man, and we know you care greatly for him, but he is still a white man."

"Why should that be important?" asked Sweet Grass.

"Your father and I have lived long enough to know that these trappers, especially white trappers, cannot be trusted." Sweet Grass gave a slow sigh, but her mother gently put her hand on her shoulder to calm her. "Raging Bull is one of our dearest friends and his heart is good without question, and maybe the same goes for He Who Walks Tall," she said. "But they are the exceptions, compared to most of their kind."

"Maybe He Who Walks Tall is the only exception I need," said Sweet Grass. "My heart belongs to him, not his entire race." Clay Basket chuckled. "Mother, how did you know that father was the right one for you?" asked Sweet Grass.

Before her mother could answer, her father spoke as he was just getting up from his buffalo robes. "I gave your grandfather ten fine horses for your mother's hand," he blurted out. Clay Basket just gave her husband a sarcastic look as he chuckled while getting dressed to head out to the lake to wash himself up, but not before giving his son a swift kick in the rump to wake him out of bed, just as the sun was finally coming up.

———

Later that afternoon, near the Yellowstone River, Azariah Hancock was just waking up to a splitting headache and very sore ribs. "Praise Jesus, Mary, Martha, and Joseph!" shouted Liam O'Reilly. "For a minute there, I thought you were gone beaver."

"What happened?" asked Azariah. "I feel like a whale just fell on me."

The Irishman chuckled. "More like Old Ephraim, after you put a hole the size of grapeshot into his chest." Suddenly the youth remembered the grizzly bear and nearly popped out of his blanket, regretting it as he grabbed his ribs. "Just rest, lad," said Liam. "I didn't feel any broken bones, but that was one huge beastie you killed that fell on top of you." As Azariah lay back down, he felt Gideon licking all over his face. The boy raised his head a little to check the pup and noticed some cuts near his ribs. "The dog was lucky," said Liam. "You need to work on him a little more, so he can learn to obey your commands better." The youth just nodded and relaxed again. "You hungry, lad?" asked Liam.

"Starving," said Azariah. "What you cooking?"

The Irishman smiled. "Grizzly stew!"

20

In less than two weeks, Azariah was back on his feet. Gideon took a little bit longer to get back to his normal self after the bear attack, but he came along nicely and didn't slack in his duties as a guard dog. Azariah and Liam continued to trap along the Yellowstone River and managed to get over two hundred pounds of beaver pelts. By near the end of the fall trapping season, they headed back to Liam's cabin in the Beartooth Mountains to retrieve their cache of pelts. They were already planning for the spring trapping season when they got back to the cabin. To Azariah's delight, the Irishman decided that they were going to trap in the Wind River Mountain Range in Shoshone country. It just so happened they would be near White Antelope's village. Although the Shoshone were historically friendly to trappers, they were longtime enemies of the Arapahoe Nation, which could mean some trouble for the duo.

However, Liam had had some dealings with the Shoshone, and many of them considered him a friend and ally despite his friendship with the Arapahoe and also an adopted Cheyenne, who were also not exactly on good speaking terms with the Shoshone.

A couple of days after returning to the cabin, Azariah had

finished tanning the grizzly bear hide. Considering how difficult it was due to the size of the great beast, the youth was very proud of his work. The Irishman had taught him well and was very impressed with Azariah's handiwork after inspecting it.

"I have a present for you, lad," said Liam. He handed Azariah a necklace made out of what appeared to be claws—grizzly bear claws. "Among the tribes, it is considered great medicine when a man kills such a huge beast."

The boy smiled as he accepted the gift. His eyes were almost watery, since other than the teachings that the Irishman had given him, along with his friendship, this was the first real gift he had ever received from him.

"Thank you, Liam," he said. "I will wear it with pride."

Liam smirked. "You better, lad. It is a symbol of bravery and honor." Azariah thought for a moment and remembered what the Oglala Lakota medicine man, High Cloud, told him about faith, honor, and even courage. He took what Liam said to heart and immediately wrapped the grizzly bear claw necklace around his neck.

Liam looked outside at the clouds. It was the middle of November, and the weather was getting colder by the minute. It wouldn't be long before winter came, and in the mountains, it could come unexpectedly. "We better start packing up the plews and getting ready for tomorrow," said Liam.

"Where we going tomorrow?" asked Azariah.

Liam gave a smile. "The Wind River Mountains to find good trapping grounds for the spring trapping season and to find White Antelope's village."

Azariah was jumping like a kid in a candy store. "Really?" he shouted. "We're going to find Sweet Grass' people?"

"Jesus, lad, it's nothing to get excited about," laughed Liam. "But yes, we are, and we're going to spend the winter with them, that's if it is okay with White Antelope."

Azariah gave a loud whoop, because he was going to see Sweet

Grass and maybe, possibly, ask her if she would be his wife, that is if her father didn't scalp him first.

"You're really in love with that girl, aren't you?" asked Liam.

Azariah turned red, almost embarrassed, but he nodded. "She is all I think about," he said. "I mean, there is something about her that makes me feel... I don't know what it is."

"Complete?"

The youth nodded. Liam gave a smile and turned his attention outside to the forest. At the entrance were the graves of his beloved Rain Cloud and infant daughter, Constance. A sense of sadness came over him as he remembered the short, happy life he had with his young family before the Crow war party took them from him. He knew what the boy was feeling and almost envied him. "I know how you feel, lad," he said. "I know it all too well."

A few weeks later, around the second week of December, the village of White Antelope was buzzing. Located in the southern range of the Wind River Mountains, everyone was getting on with their everyday life. Like their allies the Cheyenne and the Lakota, the Arapahoe tribe had prepared well for the upcoming winter and stored enough food to prevent starvation. However, that didn't mean anyone was idle. Two Hawks had just successfully led a hunt for a herd of elk a couple of days previous and many in the village were grateful for the extra meat, especially the elderly who could no longer hunt or care for themselves. Two Hawks and Howling Wolf graciously shared the spoils of the hunt with them. Warriors and hunters who were known for their selfless generosity were well respected, which was one of the reasons many of the younger men looked up to the Arapahoe elder and sub-chief. White Antelope was chief of this village because he was a born leader, but he was also wise and a good judge of character, which was why he and Two Hawks were like brothers. They both were known to put the interests of the people before their own.

It was during the cold afternoon that Sweet Grass decided to take a walk to the lake to fill her buffalo gourd for the elk stew dinner her mother was planning on making. It was at the lake where she heard a dog barking, coming from the opposite side of the lake. When she looked up, that is when she saw them and gave a huge whoop. She recognized one of the riders coming around the lake following the dog. Azariah on his black stallion was riding as fast as he could while pulling a string of pack horses with him. The faithful dog, Gideon was running along beside his master, barking and yipping as if he were excited to be coming home.

Liam, who was riding his brown pinto stallion and pulling his string of packhorses filled with an entire fall and winter season of beaver pelts, rode at a measured pace. Unlike his much younger friend and protégé, he was in no rush to get to the village. But then again, he didn't have an Arapahoe Juliet waiting on him, whom he saw running around the lake towards Azariah. The Irishman laughed when he saw Azariah pull his animals to a stop and jump off his horse to greet Sweet Grass. The girl jumped on the giant teenager, attempting to tackle him, but instead settled for a bear hug. When Liam caught up with the young lovebirds, he noticed Sweet Grass was smiling but had tears in her eyes.

"What the devil did you do, lad?" he asked.

Azariah looked up and smiled at his friend and mentor. "I told her that I am going to ask her father for her hand in marriage," he said. "That's if she welcomes me as a husband."

Liam immediately looked at Sweet Grass and could tell by her expression that there was no question. She welcomed Azariah to be her husband. "I would say congratulations, lad," said Liam. "But now you got to do the hard part first."

"Which would be?"

"Getting her daddy to say yes," said Liam as he looked beyond the young couple and noticed that the villagers were approaching, led by Chief White Antelope and none other than Two Hawks himself. "Ah, speak of the devil!"

21

Later that evening in the lodge of Sweet Grass' family, Azariah, Liam, Two Hawks, and Howling Wolf had just finished eating their dinner. Clay Basket and Sweet Grass sat in the background, finishing their dinners as well, as they listened intently for the discussion that was about to happen. Azariah and Sweet Grass had just announced their engagement to her parents, and Two Hawks was the opposite of happy. While just arriving, Azariah had asked the elder's permission for his daughter's hand in marriage. Two Hawks didn't say no, but he didn't say yes either. Sensing the tension, White Antelope and Wandering Bear silently suggested to Two Hawks that maybe he and his family should eat first, before giving his answer to something as big and serious as marriage. Clay Basket agreed and managed to convince her husband that the chief and the medicine man were right.

Azariah and Liam were invited and told that they would discuss Azariah and Sweet Grass after dinner. Liam thought it wise, and Azariah felt there was nothing wrong in waiting until after dinner, especially after seeing Two Hawks' expression when he told him about the recent engagement between himself and his daughter.

Azariah felt he was about to be led to the gallows, but at least once everyone had their bellies full, he could explain man to man to his future father-in-law of his commitment and undying love for his daughter.

"So, you wish to marry my daughter?" asked Two Hawks. The man was straightforward and saw no reason to drag this out any longer, now that everyone had eaten their fill. Azariah nodded. Two Hawks paused for a second and turned to his wife and daughter. Seeing the concerned look on Clay Basket, the Arapaho elder sensed that she shared his feelings on this subject. Sweet Grass momentarily looked at her father and smiled before bowing her head. Two Hawks already knew what was on her mind and it brought him very little comfort. He turned back to Azariah, who never took his eyes off the elder.

"What do you have to offer for her hand?" asked Two Hawks.

The moment of truth, the youth thought to himself, before answering in the Arapaho tongue. "I have three fine horses, given to me by a great Cheyenne warrior and friend named Spotted Eagle."

Two Hawks was unimpressed. "Why would a Cheyenne warrior give you three fine horses?"

"I saved his eldest son's life from a rampaging buffalo," answered Azariah.

"He Who Walks Tall speaks with a straight tongue Two Hawks," said Liam. "I know the Cheyenne warrior called Spotted Eagle personally, for he is the brother of my dead wife."

Two Hawks and Howling Wolf were convinced, for they knew Liam O'Reilly would never lie, especially about something as serious as that. Knowing that, Two Hawks began to have second thoughts about Azariah, but only a little bit.

"Two Hawks," said Azariah. "I know you don't trust me very much because I am a white man and I, for one, do not blame you." At that statement, the elder raised an eyebrow, a sign that the giant white boy got his attention. "But I speak with a straight tongue when I say that I love your daughter, and I will do everything in my power to make her happy as you love her mother and would do and have done the same for her."

A giggle from both Clay Basket and Sweet Grass caught Two Hawks' attention. It was clear to him that his wife was impressed with Azariah's flattery.

"I believe you are a good man, He Who Walks Tall," said Two Hawks. "But three horses are not enough."

Temporarily dejected, Azariah quickly regained his composure. "Name your price, and I will gladly pay it."

"Ten horses for my daughter's hand," said Two Hawks.

Azariah looked at Sweet Grass for a moment, ignoring the surprised look on Liam's face, then smiled.

"Done," he said. "I will bring you ten horses, plus the three that I already have to give."

Thirteen horses, Two Hawks thought. "How generous."

With that being said, Liam slowly moved to the youth's ear and whispered, "Just where are you going to get ten horses?"

Azariah turned and asked, "You feel like going on a horse raiding expedition against the Crow?"

The Irishman smiled.

Azariah, with the help of Howling Wolf, Beaver, and Otter Tail, along with Liam, was planning on leading a horse raiding expedition into Crow country, but a blizzard invaded the valley and made traveling impossible. Considering that it was winter, no one was surprised, but that didn't much help the situation for Azariah and Sweet Grass. Despite this, Liam and Wandering Bear cautioned patience, believing such a delay was a blessing in disguise since it gave the two more time to get to know each other and continue their courtship, under the watchful eye of Two Hawks, of course.

Azariah was determined to prove that he would be a worthy husband to Sweet Grass and earn her parents' trust. He would sometimes get up early in the morning and help bring in firewood for Sweet Grass' family or for some elder who needed some help around their lodge. He, along with Gideon, Beaver, and Otter Tail would go and check on the horses and see that they were looked after during the cold winter months. Azariah would even feed Sweet Grass' horse and the horses belonging to the rest of her family, just out of sheer courtesy.

The blizzard lasted a few days and when it subsided, Azariah went to talk to Howling Wolf, Beaver, and Otter Tail. "Now that the storm is gone, may I suggest we go hunting to bring in the meat before we pay the Crow a visit?"

"Excellent suggestion, brother," said Howling Wolf. "Even though we still have enough meat for the village to last the rest of the winter, it never hurts to have extra."

"I agree," said Otter Tail. "I would rather be doing that than being stuck in the lodge all winter like some grizzly bear in hibernation." The foursome laughed as Liam, White Antelope, Two Hawks, and Wandering Bear approached them after exiting the main lodge that held the village council. Howling Wolf told them their plans and when the older man offered to join them, none of the younger men objected.

"Thank you greatly," said Azariah. "The more experienced men we have, the greater success the hunt will be."

"Spoken like one of the people," said Wandering Bear with a smile.

Two Hawks wasn't entirely impressed, considering that the whole plan was Azariah's idea, but he wasn't against it and was very pleased that his future son-in-law had the people's welfare at heart and not for selfish reasons.

By noon, all eight men were on the trail. Despite his advanced age at fifty summers, Wandering Bear still had the vitality of a man twenty years younger. He was not only a holy man or village medicine man but also their best tracker when it came to hunting game or the enemy. Beaver was Wandering Bear's pupil and was learning how to become a tracker like the medicine man. Everything the elder did, the youth paid close attention to.

They had recently found the tracks of a moose herd. It was too early for the mating season for the moose, so it was more than likely a bull and his harem. The Arapahoe holy man and his young apprentice counted at least twenty animals from the tracks, and they were very close. Using sign language, Wandering Bear informed White Antelope and the group before he and Beaver continued. Moose was the largest of the deer family in North America. The Western Moose the men were hunting, was and still is considered the second largest of the subspecies followed by the Alaskan Moose, which is the largest. Males stood up to six feet, six inches at the shoulder, and weighed up to sixteen hundred pounds. Females are shorter and smaller, standing up to five feet, six inches at the shoulder, and weighing up to eight hundred pounds. Either way, with that many animals in the herd the men were hunting, that was a lot of meat, enough to last to the summer, let alone to the end of winter.

When they caught up to them, Azariah was amazed at the size of even the females. Granted, they weren't as big as the buffalo, but the moose was a formidable animal and just as dangerous when cornered or provoked. It was clear to everyone in the group caution must be heeded. There were calves in the herd, as well. Liam quietly counted at least eight calves, eleven adult cows, and of course, there was the bull—the king of the forest and his harem. The Irishman almost snickered as the bull strutted along the perimeter, protecting his females and young like he was the cock of the walk. Liam had seen such behavior among his fellow men, both white and red alike, and would often wonder how mankind hadn't been wiped off the face of the earth already. *Perhaps God does have a sense of humor,* he thought.

"I think we should hunt the cows that don't have young," suggested Wandering Bear through sign.

No one objected because the suggestion made a lot of sense. The village wasn't starving yet, so hunting cows with calves would be unnecessary. Under normal or extreme conditions, most men, both white and red alike, wouldn't discriminate between hunting a mother moose or calf. As the saying went in the mountains, meat is meat.

Getting Azariah's attention, Beaver and Howling Wolf pointed to two adult cows that were by themselves. They were grazing closer to the hunters than the rest of the herd. The men considered this good fortune and were not about to throw away this opportunity. The two adult females seemed to be larger than average, weighing almost as much as the bull.

Taking his Pennsylvania rifle, Azariah quickly aimed at the one closest to him and cocked the rifle. By the time the moose cow heard the click, it was too late. Azariah pulled the trigger and *BOOM*! She was dead before she even hit the ground. The second female, who was grazing with her, bolted but not before Beaver put two arrows into her. Liam fired his Pennsylvania rifle into a third cow that was near the herd. She dropped in the middle of the run as the herd bolted. Beaver and Otter Tail chased the second moose cow on their horses, and Otter Tail managed to thrust his lance into the beast before she collapsed. By the time it was all over, there were three dead adult moose cows, ready to be skinned, gutted, and over twenty-four-hundred pounds of meat to be transported back to the village on a travois.

"Today is a good day," said White Antelope as he, Liam, Two Hawks, and Wandering Bear approached one of the carcasses. Howling Wolf was sent back to get the rest of the horses to start carrying the bounty, while the rest of the men quickly dismounted and started butchering their prize.

22

When the hunting party returned to the village, there was great excitement over the sight of what they brought home. It was clear to everyone how successful the hunt was by just looking at the large amounts of moose meat that was brought in on the travois. Azariah gave half of his share of the meat to Two Hawks and Howling Wolf. The rest he gave to the elderly who were no longer able to hunt for their food. This act of generosity didn't go unnoticed and was praised by Liam, White Antelope, and Wandering Bear. Even Two Hawks was impressed and somehow mellowed a bit towards the young white boy.

As Clay Basket and Sweet Grass were preparing dinner, Two Hawks pulled Azariah aside, wishing to speak to him privately. "You have proven once again to be an honorable man, He Who Walks Tall," he said.

"Thank you, Two Hawks," responded Azariah.

The elder and the youth decided to go for a walk near the lake. Azariah knew that his future father-in-law had something on his mind but chose to let him break the ice.

"You understand my concern?" asked Two Hawks.

"About me and your daughter?" The elder nodded. Azariah sighed before continuing. "I understand your concern, that you don't want your daughter to be married to a white man, and I do not blame you."

Two Hawks pondered for a moment. "I want my daughter to be safe," he said. "But I also want her to be happy."

Azariah smiled at that. "I pray that I am worthy to be the man to make her happy," he said. "I have never been in love before, and I have prayed to God to help me not be a man who would cause pain to someone I love dearly."

"You speak as you are familiar with hurt when it comes to the heart," said Two Hawks. It was clear that the elder hit the nail on the head with that statement.

"I know what it is like to have someone inflict pain on someone you love dearly."

This got Two Hawks' attention. "Tell me more," he said.

Azariah told about what happened to his twin sister and exacting revenge against the man who caused her great pain. He told about why he was forced to leave his family and flee out West. He explained that meeting Liam O'Reilly and learning from him was a lifesaver and probably the best thing to ever happen to him since he was forced to leave his home. That was until he met Sweet Grass. "So, you understand that I wouldn't—or couldn't—intentionally cause Sweet Grass any kind of pain or dishonor her in any way, because I know what it is like to have that happen."

"Hmm," grunted Two Hawks. "I am glad you told me this." Two Hawks gently put his arm across Azariah's shoulder as they continued to walk. "Do you miss your family?"

"Very much so," answered Azariah. "But I can only pray and hope that God has them in His hands."

"You speak very highly about your God," said Two Hawks with a sense of curiosity. "The one you call Jesus Christ."

"My father is a holy man, like Wandering Bear," said Azariah. "He believes that the one we call Jesus Christ created the earth in six days and rested on the seventh, and that all of mankind are descendants of the first man and woman."

Two Hawks thought for a moment as he pondered what the youth just told him about his religious beliefs. "We have a similar belief in a way," he said. "We believe that we are all created equal by the Man Above and that we are all related."

"Raging Bull told me about that," said Azariah. "He mentioned that the Cheyenne and the Lakota practice the same belief too."

"And you?" asked Two Hawks. "What do you believe in?"

Azariah pondered that question for a moment, before answering. "I know I haven't been here long, but what I have learned, I believe that who I call Jesus Christ and who you call The Man Above, are the same." The Arapahoe elder raised an eyebrow as if very interested in Azariah's reasoning. "Don't ask me how, but I find there are more similarities between our religious beliefs than there are differences," said Azariah. "It goes to show that your people and my people have a lot more in common than we are willing to admit."

"I cannot argue with that," said Two Hawks.

"However, I think the only difference is that the Arapahos, or even most of the tribes that I have come in contact with, don't judge a man by his skin color, unlike my people do," said Azariah.

Two Hawks smirked and said, "Now that I strongly will not argue with."

With that, Azariah laughed as he realized that he and his future father-in-law somehow managed to come to common ground and even friendship developed as they walked back to the village.

On their way back is when they noticed something in the forest. A slight movement appeared to be a man crawling towards them. Two Hawks and Azariah, both armed, went to investigate and as they approached, their suspicions were correct. It was a man, but a white man half-frozen and looked like he hadn't eaten in a while.

"Help me," said the stranger. His voice was weak and he wore a grizzly bear hide. His hair was long and black as well as his beard, which was covered in snow and frost from bottom to top.

"Stay here with him, while I will bring help," said Two Hawks.

Azariah stayed with the stranger, but something did not feel right, as if a sixth sense was telling Azariah that it would be best to leave this man to the wolves, but at the same time, his Christian upbringing couldn't allow him to abandon someone in need. Either way, the youth gently lifted the stranger and gave him a piece of beef jerky and some water, until Two Hawks returned. "What is your name, sir?" asked Azariah.

The stranger looked up at the youth and weakly answered, "Manson. John Manson."

"Help is on the way, John," said Azariah. "You're among friends."

Little did he know at that moment, Azariah would come to regret that and realize that his sixth sense had been correct.

23

They were able to bring the half-frozen stranger called John Manson to the village. Wandering Bear's daughter, Black Shawl, was an expert healer and mixed some herbs in boiling water that would warm the newcomer slowly but surely. Her ten-year-old daughter, Laughing Bird, and her husband, Night Wing, managed to cover the newcomer with two or three buffalo robes to warm him up as she and her father tried to get the healing herbal tea into the man.

Word reached Liam O'Reilly and White Antelope that Azariah and Two Hawks brought in the stranger who was now at the lodge of Night Wing and Black Shawl. They came to the lodge followed by Clay Basket, Howling Wolf, Sweet Grass, Otter Tail, and Beaver, and some other members of the head council.

"Brought in a stray, huh, lad?" asked Liam. "How bad is he?"

The youth just shrugged. "He was nearly half-frozen from the looks of it, plus, he looked like he had not eaten in days."

Liam thought for a moment. "What did you say his name was?"

"He said his name was Manson," answered Azariah. "John Manson."

"Something bothering you, lad?" asked Liam.

Azariah wasn't sure what was bothering him, but he felt an instinct in his gut that saving the stranger's life was a mistake. "You know of a trapper or anyone by the name of John Manson?"

"Can't say that I do," answered Liam.

"What are your thoughts, He Who Walks Tall?" asked Two Hawks in Arapaho.

"I am not sure," answered Azariah in the same tongue. "I have a bad feeling about the stranger." Azariah's statement caught everyone's attention.

"You believe that you shouldn't have brought him to our village?" asked White Antelope.

The youth nodded. "I can't say why, and I almost feel ashamed for even thinking it, since none of us know this man."

"It is never wrong to be cautious, He Who Walks Tall," said Two Hawks. "A man has to know his own mind and trust his own instincts."

"In other words, lad," added Liam, "listen to what your gut tells you."

Azariah took the advice to heart. Night Wing and Laughing Bird exited the lodge and announced that the man called John Manson was resting. Wandering Bear and Black Shawl were with him and checking on his progress. With that, White Antelope suggested the crowd disperse and leave the medicine man and his daughter to their work.

Azariah filed his suspicions about John Manson in the back of his mind. The fact that he and Two Hawks had come to an understanding and that the elder had now accepted him as a future son-in-law brought the giant youth great joy. He and Sweet Grass continued their courtship this time without supervision, which made everything a whole lot easier.

It was the beginning of the new year in the second week of January. Azariah, now fifteen, was anxious about his upcoming wedding. He told his plans of the horse raiding expedition against the Crow to Liam, Two Hawks, Howling Wolf, Beaver, and Otter Tail. He thought doing it in the middle of winter was sound because most tribes of the plains do not raid each other in the wintertime. No one, not even Two Hawks, argued against it. It was just the opposite. The Crow would never suspect it, not during the middle of winter.

However, something else was making the youth anxious. John Manson had recovered quickly from his ordeal. He told Liam and Azariah that he was a free trapper like themselves and that he used to work for American Fur Company back East near Lake Michigan. He had come west for better trapping grounds and more freedom about four years ago. Azariah suspected that there was more to the story than what Manson was letting on.

Liam, Two Hawks, Sweet Grass, and Howling Wolf shared his suspicions, yet nobody had any proof that the newcomer was dangerous or had ill intentions. During the previous few weeks, he helped with the hunting and even helped Wandering Bear's family with their chores around their lodge and often volunteered to help keep watch on the horses against horse thieves from enemy tribes.

Manson wasn't a talkative person. He was six-foot-two, weighed about two hundred pounds or less, had brown hair and brown eyes, and appeared to be in his late thirties. Liam and Azariah noticed a Southern accent, so even though they didn't ask where he was from, they suspected that he was from the deep South. Azariah learned during his short time in the West that there was an unwritten rule among trappers: "Mind your own business." Still, Azariah's bad feeling about Manson wouldn't go away, and he prayed that he was wrong about him.

He shared these feelings with Sweet Grass, and she mentioned that she, too, didn't trust the newcomer. "I don't like the way he looks at some of the girls here," she said.

That statement took Azariah off guard. "What do you mean, the girls?"

"The young girls, around Laughing Bird's age."

Azariah started to get concerned. "Have you told your father this or White Antelope?"

Sweet Grass slowly shook her head. "I see how he looks at Laughing Bird," she said. "He is very subtle about it so that no one will notice it."

"You did, obviously," said Azariah. "We better tell Wandering Bear and Night Wing at least."

"I agree."

Later that day, they found Wandering Bear by Chief White Antelope's lodge, talking with the leader, along with Liam and Two Hawks. They expressed their concerns about John Manson and were surprised to know that the medicine man shared their distrust of the trapper as well. However, he admitted that he didn't notice the trapper's subtle lustful looks towards his granddaughter.

"It is not my place to say this," said Liam in the Arapahoe tongue. "But I believe the man has overstayed his welcome."

Two Hawks agreed. "If what my daughter and He Who Walks Tall say are true, then it is time for him to leave."

"But he hasn't done anything wrong," said White Antelope. "Not yet, at least."

"If I may speak, Chief White Antelope?" asked Azariah.

The chief gave the youth permission to speak.

"I believe he should leave before he does do something wrong," said Azariah. "From what Sweet Grass just told me, this man is dangerous, especially around little girls. He may not show it and is very crafty and subtle about it, which makes him even more dangerous, and that is what worries me."

From the expression on the youth's face, Wandering Bear suspected that there was more to the reasoning that led to Azariah's worries. "You have known men like him before, He Who Walks Tall?"

"Unfortunately, I have," said Azariah. "My twin sister was raped by men like him."

That was all the medicine man needed to hear, and he headed

back towards his lodge to talk to his daughter and son-in-law about their guest.

"I hope I am wrong about this," Azariah said.

Liam, Two Hawks, Chief White Antelope, and Sweet Grass nodded in agreement, but all of them knew that Azariah probably was not wrong.

24

By the time Wandering Bear returned to his lodge, he found his granddaughter, Laughing Bird, weeping, while Black Shawl tried to comfort her. "What has happened?" he asked.

Black Shawl was hesitant to tell her father but managed to find the strength. "The white man, Manson," was all she said.

Wandering Bear fell to his knees and gently put his hands on his granddaughter's shoulders. "Did he touch you?" Laughing Bird just nodded. "Tell me more, granddaughter," he said. "Do not be afraid."

"I was playing down by the lake near the horses," said Laughing Bird. "He said that he saw a pretty butterfly and wanted to show me near the bushes, and that is when he grabbed and he hurt me."

"Did you try to scream?" asked Wandering Bear.

"He said he would kill me and my parents and you if I tried to scream or if I told anyone," answered Laughing Bird.

It took all the self-control that Wandering Bear had to keep his rage in check.

"Have you told Night Wing?" he asked his daughter.

"Not yet."

"Tell him when he returns from his hunt and then have him meet me at Two Hawks' lodge."

When word of what John Manson did to little Laughing Bird spread around the entire village, everyone's bloodlust was up, but no more than Night Wing and Wandering Bear. However, before they could get their hands on the child molester, John Manson managed to escape by stealing one of the horses from the herd.

Standing before the council, Night Wing was planning on getting a revenge party together to hunt down the rapist, when Azariah entered and volunteered to go with him.

"This is all my fault, Night Wing," he said. "I suspected Manson's treachery from the beginning, and I brought him among your people when I should have left him to die where I found him."

Night Wing was enraged, but he didn't blame Azariah nor Two Hawks, for that matter, since the elder was with the youth when they found John Manson, brought him in and helped nurse him back to health.

"What's done is done, He Who Walks Tall," he said. "No one could have honestly known what that man would do, but what matters now is that he pays for what he has done."

"I agree," said Liam O'Reilly, who also volunteered his services to hunt down John Manson. "He couldn't have gone far, considering that there is still snow on the ground, and from what I saw from the clouds today, another snowstorm is coming and soon."

"Then we have little time to waste," said Wandering Bear.

It took the revenge party no less than half an hour to get ready. Azariah had Gideon sniff out Manson's trail. That gave them an advantage over the fugitive.

Before riding out of the village, Liam strode over to Azariah to reassure him. "This isn't your fault, lad," he said. "As Night Wing said, no one could have known what that sick bastard was planning."

Azariah turned and gave his mentor a look that the Irishman had seen among men who were on a mission of blood. "Tell that to Night Wing's daughter."

Gideon picked up the scent and led the hunting party towards John Manson. The rapist had at least a two-hour head start but still couldn't get very far in knee-deep snow. He suspected that Laughing Bird had told her parents what he did to her, and he was not under any delusions of what fate had in store for him if the Arapahos caught up to him. Fortunately for him, he still had his own Pennsylvania rifle and powder horn. Manson figured that if he couldn't outrun them, he could find a good look-out spot and cut down the odds in his favor a bit.

He managed to find high ground and a cave. *Good place to make a stand*, he thought. John Manson was never a man who thought things through before doing things, good or bad. After raping his twelve-year-old niece over a decade ago, the illegitimate son of a plantation owner was forced to flee his Columbia, South Carolina home, rather than face the wrath of his half-brother. Not that he cared much about his family or anyone else other than himself. His father didn't give him much love, since he was the offspring of a fling between his wealthy father and the town pastor's wayward daughter. His stepmother and older half-siblings were worse. Even though his father claimed him, that was all he would do for him and left him with nothing in his will. When his eldest half-brother offered to hire him as an overseer on the plantation, deep down John Manson felt insulted and believed he deserved more than that, a lot more. Violating his niece was the ultimate revenge against not just his half-brother, but against the whole family for the mistreatment against him his entire life. Since then, John Manson had walked that road as if he were entitled to anything and everything, and nobody better get in his way.

Even when he signed on to trap for the American Fur Company, he raised a lot of hell in the Lake Michigan region after he assaulted two American Indian girls. His employers felt that he was a liability, so they offered to surrender him to the tribe of the two victims. But he escaped justice again and found himself in St. Louis, where he joined a group of successful French trappers. However, his pompous attitude got him in trouble with them, and they abandoned him near Independence Rock, with no horse. He walked and crawled until his body damn near gave out on him, and it was near the village of White Antelope in the Wind River Mountains that Azariah Hancock and Two Hawks found him.

Unsurprisingly, John Manson shared the view of most whites that Indians were inferior, but he wasn't a complete idiot. He knew or suspected that the giant white teenager and his dumb Irish prick of a mentor didn't trust him. Not that he cared anyway. He wouldn't have been surprised if they were among the hunting party trailing him, to either kill him or bring him back to face justice. "The joke is on you," he silently said to himself. "Damned Injun lovers!" He was waiting patiently from his hide-out, already decided that if Hancock and the Irishman were with their Injun friends, he would take them out first.

"He is close," said Azariah.

"How do you know, lad?" asked Liam.

The youth pointed to Gideon, who had stopped and gave a low growl.

Liam knew that their quarry was close; he was just testing his friend and protégé. Night Wing, Wandering Bear, and Two Hawks also knew that John Manson was close and suspected that he was planning an ambush of some sort.

"His tracks lead that way," said Liam in the Arapaho tongue. "It appears he has the high ground and can pick us off one by one."

"You have a plan, Raging Bull?" asked Night Wing.

Liam nodded. "I think it is best if we split up, and since there are ten of us, we should do it in three groups." Night Wing and Two Hawks decided to ride with Azariah, while Wandering Bear and Howling Wolf rode with Liam. The last four warriors were Beaver, Otter Tail, and two named Red Lance and Elk Horn.

The men doubled back on their tracks and managed to circle their quarry in different directions. Night Wing, Two Hawks, and Azariah went north; Wandering Bear, Howling Wolf, and Liam went south; and the rest of the men took a western route to surprise the fugitive. It was agreed by everyone that John Manson was to be taken alive if possible and brought back to the village to face justice for what he has done. However, that didn't mean Night Wing liked it, for he wanted to kill the sick bastard for raping his daughter and he wasn't alone in that thinking.

Feeling completely responsible for saving John Manson's life and bringing him into their village, Azariah wanted to skin the rapist alive. The youth also had a personal reason for wanting to kill John Manson, a reason that Two Hawks could only guess by his expression. Azariah was thinking of his twin sister, Abigail, and what was done to her. John Manson's sick treachery brought back that painful memory, and it was too much for the giant youth to handle.

Gideon gave another low growl as a signal to his master that they were close. Azariah patted the dog on his head and signed to Two Hawks that he should stay behind with the animal, while Night Wing and he climbed up the cliff to have a look-see. The elder did not object but reminded the two that Manson was to be brought back alive. Both men nodded before moving on.

Azariah checked his Pennsylvania rifle and two pistols to see if they were loaded and primed. Night Wing had his bow and arrows, along with two scalping knives and a tomahawk ready. When they reached their objective, they found their prey, who was waiting from his hiding place, prepared to set up his ambush. Little did he know that at least two of his pursuers were right behind him, actually right above him, ready to pounce. The sound of Azariah's rifle being cocked caught John Manson's attention, but too late.

"Drop your weapons, you sick bastard," shouted Azariah as he aimed his rifle at the fugitive. "Or so help me God, you will find yourself in Hell real quick!"

Realizing he was outgunned, the fugitive tried to buy some time. "You wouldn't shoot a fellow white man in the back?"

Despite the fact he had just turned fifteen years old a couple of weeks prior, Azariah was not a fool nor naïve. "In a heartbeat!"

"I can't believe you would turn in a white man to these heathens," said Manson. "And over a stinking squaw!"

Noticing the rapist trying to sneak out a pistol while dropping his rifle, Azariah shot him in his left ankle without hesitation. John Manson howled in pain as Night Wing pounced on him in time to put a knife to his throat. Manson could see the rage in the man's eyes and also noticed that the warrior was using all the self-control he had to keep from cutting his throat.

Azariah immediately jumped down and was standing right beside Night Wing as he pulled out one pistol and pointed it at John Manson's temple. "Please give us an excuse," he said with venom.

Realizing he was in a no-win situation, John Manson surrendered. Night Wing took all his weapons and made sure he was completely unarmed. Azariah fired one of his pistols in the air to signal to the rest of the hunting party that they got their quarry. Suddenly, Gideon showed up with Two Hawks and managed to come between his master and John Manson, growling at the latter.

"Gideon," said Azariah, "he makes a move, rip his throat out."

For the first time, John Manson was terrified and it showed when he quickly pissed himself.

When Liam and the rest of the party showed up and gathered around John Manson, they had him stripped butt naked and tied his hands behind his back. He demanded that his wound be tended to, but the Irishman gave him a smirk and said, "Your ankle wound is the least of your problems now. Pretty soon it won't even matter."

"Piss on you, you dumb potato-eating mick," responded Manson, trying to show some bravado.

Liam responded with a quick right hook to the man's jaw, knocking him senseless. "You know, I see no reason why you can't deliver justice right here and now," said Liam to Night Wing and Wandering Bear. "It was your daughter and granddaughter that he violated."

"As much as I want to kill him now, Raging Bull," said Night

Wing, "it would be too good for him and merciful, compared to what our women will do to him."

"I agree," said Wandering Bear. "What we could do to him cannot compare."

"As long as I get to watch," added Azariah.

Night Wing and some of the warriors looked at the youth with a little surprise. However, Two Hawks, Liam, and Wandering Bear understood his anger, for they knew about what happened to his sister and guessed that what John Manson did to Laughing Bird brought back that painful memory.

A couple of hours later, they returned to the village with their prisoner. John Manson was gagged by Azariah, to keep him from hurling insults at everyone. Night Wing took the prisoner by the rawhide rope tied around his neck and dragged him over to the center of the village, where he was staked down, spread-eagled. As soon as the gag was removed, Manson continued to spit out insults and curses, mostly towards Azariah and Liam, for selling out a white man to these heathens.

This was more than Azariah could tolerate. "You don't get it, do you?" he asked the condemned prisoner. "You raped a child, a ten-year-old child!"

John Manson scoffed. "She was woman enough for me. Besides, she was only a dirty Injun brat!"

Suddenly, Azariah gave out a huge roar that would've done justice to an angry she-grizzly and immediately took out his Arkansas toothpick, grabbed John Manson by the balls, and with one swipe, castrated the sick bastard. The doomed rapist screamed like a banshee and would have continued to do so, had not Azariah shoved the man's severed shaft and testicles down his throat. Azariah was about to do more, but Liam and Wandering Bear quickly pulled him away from John Manson.

"You have done enough, lad," said Liam. "Let the women do the rest."

Azariah tried to fight his mentor but calmed himself down when

Sweet Grass stood in front of him and touched his cheek. Like an iceberg cooling down an erupting volcano, Azariah allowed himself to be guided to the lake by his love to help wash the blood from his hands. As this was going on, the women of the village of White Antelope, led by Black Shawl, were delivering justice to John Manson, who screamed in extreme agony as they skinned him alive.

25

The next couple of days were not easy for Azariah Hancock. After justice was delivered to the vile John Manson, the expected snowstorm came to the valley. With her parents' permission, Sweet Grass invited Azariah to stay with her family, for which the youth was grateful and enjoyed her company. Despite that he was an honorable and grateful guest, it was hard for him to sleep at night since John Manson's heinous crime against poor Laughing Bird. Memories of his sister's attack plagued Azariah at night, and he would wake up in a cold sweat and would sometimes walk down to the lake, when the weather permitted, in the middle of the night to weep. Sweet Grass was some comfort, but Azariah was racked with guilt, feeling that he failed to protect his sister, and he now blamed himself for what happened to Laughing Bird.

A week later, during a chilly morning, Azariah visited Wandering Bear's family. After knocking on the flap of the medicine man's lodge, he waited until it was open and Wandering Bear poked out his head.

"Greetings, He Who Walks Tall," he said. "Please do come in."

The youth slowly entered and quickly noticed that Black Shawl,

Night Wing, and Laughing Bird were present as well. He immediately avoided looking at them, hanging his head in shame. The family quickly noticed the expression as Wandering Bear directed the youth to sit.

"What troubles you, He Who Walks Tall?" asked Wandering Bear.

Azariah suddenly looked up with tears in his eyes towards Night Wing and Black Shawl, then toward their little girl. "I am truly sorry for what that man did to Laughing Bird," he said in Arapaho. "I am to blame for it." Azariah then slowly took out his knife and handed it to Night Wing. "Your daughter would have never been violated had I not brought her attacker into your village. I, too, should be punished for what he did to her."

Before Night Wing could react, Black Shawl took the knife from her husband and gave it back to Azariah, before speaking. "You are innocent of this, He Who Walks Tall. No one could have known what was in that man's heart. What's done is done, and he paid with his life for his crime against my daughter."

"It was you who helped us capture him and brought him back to face justice," added Night Wing. "This is not on you; it was him and him alone." Wandering Bear suddenly placed a hand on Azariah's shoulder. "Tell them about your sister."

Azariah explained what happened to his sister and why he was forced to leave his home after he took vengeance on the man who raped her. "I could not protect or save my sister and now my own stupidity has caused you and your family great pain."

As Azariah buried his head in his hands, weeping, Black Shawl suddenly wrapped her arms around him in comfort, then little Laughing Bird walked up to him and hugged him as well.

"Don't cry, He Who Walks Tall. Please, don't cry."

Azariah looked into the Arapaho child's eyes and saw something he didn't expect. He saw not only forgiveness but strength, more strength than most girls her age, especially after what she just went through. She gently touched his cheek to wipe away his tears and gave a slight smile. He returned the smile and gently stroked her head.

"There is nothing for you to be sorry about," said Black Shawl. "You should not be angry with yourself for what happened to your sister or my daughter, for you are not responsible for what was done to them."

"The men responsible for the pain they caused have paid for it," said Night Wing. "Take comfort in that."

"Also take comfort that my granddaughter and your sister still live," said Wandering Bear.

Black Shawl tried to give Azariah his knife back, but he kindly refused it.

"Keep it," he said, "for Laughing Bird. She will need it more than me." He suddenly turned to Laughing Bird and pointed to the knife. "Learn how to use that and use it well, so that no one will ever attempt to force themselves on you again."

The child nodded as her parents beamed with pride.

"Now that we have that out of the way," said Wandering Bear. "Don't you have a horse raiding expedition to plan against our Crow enemies?"

For the first time, Azariah smiled, while everybody laughed.

26

It was the end of February. It would be a few weeks before spring would begin, but the winter of 1821 was still mild in the Rockies, and at least for the lovesick Azariah Hancock, it was a good day to visit the Crow and capture some Crow horses. Accompanying him were Howling Wolf, Beaver, Otter Tail, Night Wing, and of course, Liam O'Reilly. Horse raiding, like hunting buffalo on a surround, was a serious and dangerous business. Since the Crow and the Arapaho were mortal enemies since time began, it was likely this expedition would end in bloodshed. Even in the most successful horse raids, it was rare that one ended without somebody losing their life or scalp.

What made this raid so rare was that it was being done during the winter. Most horse raiding expeditions against enemy tribes took place between late spring to late summer and sometimes early fall. Azariah knew this but thought it would be a perfect and calculated opportunity that the Crow would never expect or see coming. However, he was far from naïve. Liam and Night Wing strongly advised him not to underestimate the Crow, for they were not fools either. No tribe was better at stealing or capturing horses from enemies or trappers or even their friends than the proud members of the Crow Nation.

Called the Apsáalooke, which means Crow or children of the large-beaked bird in their native tongue, they were historically known to be the practical jokers of the Northern Plains and Northern Rockies. Once established in the valley of the Yellowstone River and its tributaries on the Northern Plains in what is now known as the states of Montana and Wyoming, the Crow divided into four groups: the Mountain Crow, River Crow, Kicked in the Bellies, and Beaver Dries Its Fur.

Formerly semi-nomadic hunters and farmers in the northeastern woodland, they adapted to the nomadic lifestyle of the Plains Indians as hunters and gatherers and hunted bison. Before 1700, they were using dog travois for carrying goods. But from about 1740, the Plains tribes rapidly adopted the horse, which allowed them to move out onto the Plains and hunt buffalo more effectively. However, the severe winters in the north kept their herds smaller than those of Plains tribes in the south. The Crow, along with their cousins the Hidatsa, Eastern Shoshone, and Northern Shoshone soon became noted as horse breeders and dealers and developed relatively large horse herds. At the time, other eastern and northern tribes were also moving on to the Plains in search of a game for the fur trade, bison, and more horses. The Crow were subject to raids and horse thefts by horse-poor tribes, including the powerful Blackfoot Confederacy and their allies. Later they had to face the Lakota and their allies, the Arapaho and Cheyenne, who also stole horses from their enemies. Their greatest enemies became the tribes of the Blackfoot Confederacy and the Lakota-Cheyenne-Arapaho alliance. However, the Crow were generally friendly with the northern Plains tribes of the Flathead (although sometimes they had conflicts), Nez Perce, Kutenai, Shoshone, Kiowa, and Kiowa Apache as well as most trappers of the fur trade.

The reason why Liam O'Reilly and some trappers like him had a grudge against the Crow was mainly that they ended up marrying into enemy tribes and learned that if you marry into a tribe, their allies become your allies, and their enemies become your enemies. Despite this, some trappers managed to live peacefully between enemy tribes, but that was rare.

Azariah would always listen and take any advice that his mentor and Night Wing gave him and absorb it. He wanted this horse raiding expedition to not only be successful—after all, the whole purpose was to get ten horses as a bride price for Sweet Grass—but he had hoped that it could and would be done without bloodshed.

He mentioned that to Liam, to which the Irishman responded, "Do you believe such a thing is possible?"

The youth just shrugged. "A man can hope, but anything is possible."

Liam cackled. "Touché!"

It would take at least a couple of days to a week to reach Crow country, especially the Yellowstone region. Azariah was not taking any chances. The weather continued to be agreeable, but the giant youth learned during a short time that Mother Nature was one hundred percent unpredictable and just as lethal as any warrior from an enemy tribe or a deadly grizzly bear. Despite that, their travel was uneventful.

It was agreed that hunting for meat while going into Crow country would be done with bows and arrows instead of firearms, to not attract unwanted attention. Beaver and Otter Tail had taught Azariah how to use the bow and arrow. Like everything else he learned, Azariah became an adept student. The fourth day after leaving their village, Azariah and Beaver managed to bring down a yearling mule deer. They had plenty of pemmican and beef jerky, but that would be saved for later, once they got closer to enemy territory. The mule deer was a welcome sight and nothing was put to waste as they dried the meat and pummeled what would not be eaten that night into beef jerky and pemmican.

By the time they reached the Yellowstone River, they no longer would have fire in their camp at night. Caution and wits were the key to making this mission a success and be able to make it back home alive. Although it was colder at night than during the day, the winter weather was still mild, and everyone's spirits were high.

Early one morning, Howling Wolf and Otter Tail decided to scout ahead to see if there were any Crow villages nearby. Night Wing told them to be extra careful and not be gone too long. They assured him that all would be well, and they would return before nightfall, but the experienced warrior knew the pride of young people. A couple of years younger than Liam, Night Wing had often thought back to when he was these boys' ages, and he was always making rash decisions to try to make a name for himself. He didn't expect Howling Wolf, Otter Tail, or even Azariah to be any different.

"I worry about our youth today," he said while getting ready to be on the move again.

"What do you mean?" asked Liam.

The warrior just sighed before he answered. "I remember when I was their age, so full of vim and vigor."

"You left out arrogant, my friend," teased the Irishman.

Night Wing chuckled. "That too."

Both men glanced at Azariah and Beaver for a moment. The boys had just finished rubbing down the horses and getting them ready to travel, once Howling Wolf and Otter Tail came back from their scouting mission.

"He Who Walks Tall is a good man," said Night Wing. "He has the maturity of men much older than himself."

"He has been through a lot," added Liam. "He has seen and done things that no boy his age should ever have to do or see."

Night Wing grunted in agreement. "Same can be said for Otter Tail," said the warrior. "But I find myself worrying about He Who Walks Tall more than most of the boys of my people."

The statement caught Liam's attention. "Is it because he is white and not of the people?"

Night Wing nodded. "Don't be mistaken, Raging Bull. He Who Walks Tall is a good man. I worry *for* him, not *because* of him."

"Because of what happened to Laughing Bird and his own pain," said Liam.

Night Wing knew that was a statement and not a question. "His past haunts him," he said. "Telling him that he is not responsible for that or for what happened to my daughter will not change it."

"I never really thought of that," said Liam.

"I am surprised you didn't, my friend," responded Night Wing. "I heard how you got the name Raging Bull."

Liam glanced back at Azariah for a moment and thought about what Night Wing just said. "I see your point," he said. "What the Crow did to my family turned me into someone or something that I didn't want to become." The Irishman paused for a moment before asking Night Wing, "You think the same thing is happening to He Who Walks Tall?"

"I don't think it," said Night Wing. "I know it."

"Well, you saw how much he wanted to avenge your daughter's rape," said Liam. "I don't see that as a bad thing, though."

"Maybe it is bad, maybe not," said Night Wing. "But you and I have seen the ugliness of vengeance and what it does to a man's soul."

Liam nodded but wasn't fully convinced that Azariah would be affected by such emotion, but then again, he remembered his pain and what vengeance and guilt did to him. "Each man has to walk his own path," he said to Night Wing. "He Who Walks Tall is no different."

"Why did the Lakota medicine man, High Cloud, give him that name?" asked Night Wing.

"He saw him in a vision many years ago," answered Liam. "Said that Wakan Tanka had chosen a path for him to take and that if he chose that path, he would not walk it alone."

Night Wing was surprised. "Not walk it alone?" Then the warrior's eyes widened. "You mean Sweet Grass?"

"I am not sure, my friend," said Liam. "But all signs are pointing to her in walking that same path with He Who Walks Tall."

Now Night Wing glanced at Azariah, who along with Beaver, was having coffee. The warrior smiled. "She could do much worse than him."

27

Howling Wolf and Otter Tail returned from their scouting mission later that afternoon and reported that there was a Crow village at least ten miles or more from where they were camping. Night Wing and Liam felt this was good information and suggested they wait until nightfall to visit their enemies. Azariah, who planned this expedition, immediately agreed and had everyone pack up and head towards the village, but they would wait until nightfall to steal the Crow horses from the village herd.

About two miles out of the Crow village, it was three hours after sunset. Azariah went to a secluded spot to be alone and pray as Liam and the rest of the raiding party were getting ready.

"Lord, it has been a while since we talked," said Azariah. "First, I want to thank You for bringing me this far and protecting me; I want to thank You for new friends and for protecting them; Lord, if Sweet Grass is the one that You would have me marry, Lord, then please give me a sign and let Your will be done." As soon as he asked that question, a wolf howled at the moon from a mountain peak. Azariah smiled and said, "I assumed that is Your answer, Lord. Thank you and Amen."

The Crow village that Azariah and the Arapahoe warriors came upon was called the Kicked-in-the-Bellies. Liam suggested using knives to cut the ropes that held the herd together and, if necessary, the throats of the Crow to keep them from sounding the alarm and alerting the rest of the village. Around midnight, the men slowly and quietly walked to the horse herd.

Azariah and Howling Wolf volunteered to go first. Like stalking panthers, they slowly sneaked into the herd without spooking the horses. Armed with clubs, Beaver and Otter Tail came from the opposite direction and surprised two Crow guards, before dispatching them with their weapons. The two young warriors showed that there was no love lost for their enemy as they quietly cut the throats of the Crow guards and took their scalps, before sneaking into the horse herd themselves to join Azariah and Howling Wolf.

Liam and Night Wing stayed in the shadows to keep a lookout. Once the boys managed to hop on a Crow horse, they were to shout at the top of their lungs and that would stampede the herd. Liam and Night Wing would cover their escape from the shadows, buying them time.

At that exact moment, Azariah hopped on one horse, bareback, followed by Howling Wolf, Beaver, and Otter Tail. All four young men suddenly gave a loud yipping, which caused the herd to start stamping in a southeasterly direction away from the village. The plan had worked. The village had awakened but the Crow guards who were not killed by the intruders were completely caught off guard. Azariah and Howling Wolf led the way, as Liam and Night Wing covered their backtrail. Four Crow warriors, who saw the intruders fleeing with their herd, were cut down by rifle shots from the Irishman's gun and arrows from Night Wing's bow, in their futile attempt to stop the intruders and reclaim the herd. Liam and Night Wing managed to escape and rejoin their friends during the chaos.

About a week and a day later, the horse raiding party returned triumphantly to the Arapahoe village of White Antelope. Beaver and Otter Tail were each holding up a Crow scalp and praising Azariah and Howling Wolf, who both planned out the raid, for great success and the fact that no lives other than that of the enemy were lost. White Antelope, Two Hawks, and the rest of the council, as well as many warriors and families of Beaver and Otter Tail, beamed with pride for the coup the two young men counted on their enemies and cheered for Azariah and Howling Wolf for executing a successful horse raid.

Feeling that too much credit was heaped upon themselves, Azariah and Howling Wolf both said that the plan couldn't have worked if it weren't for Night Wing and Raging Bull, as well as Beaver and Otter Tail. Liam and Night Wing, who had been on horse raids before, were both gracious and humble in the praise but told the council that the young men deserved full credit since this was their first horse raiding expedition. Howling Wolf took it a step further when he said that the real credit should go to the Man Above. No one disagreed with him on that one. Two Hawks inspected the herd and was amazed at how large it was.

"As soon as we were safe from the Crow village," said Azariah, "we counted at least one hundred and ten horses, but we lost about twenty, two days ago."

"Still," said Two Hawks. "Bringing in ninety horses is quite an accomplishment."

"Ten of those horses are yours, Two Hawks," said Azariah. "Plus the three that I have already given you, the rest belong to Raging Bull, Night Wing, Beaver, Otter Tail, and your son."

Everyone including Liam was amazed. "We have done nothing to deserve such generosity," said Beaver.

"I disagree," said Azariah. "I could never have accomplished this on my own. Plus, I consider all of you not just friends, but family. A wise man told me once that a man's true heart is judged by how he looks after his family."

"Sound advice," said Wandering Bear. "Who is this wise man that taught you to think and behave in such a way?"

Azariah beamed with pride as he answered, "My father."

At that exact moment, Sweet Grass appeared from behind her mother, followed by Gideon. At the mere sight of her, Azariah jumped off his horse and ran to her, picking her up in a bear hug as he kissed her. She returned his affection with a loving embrace of her own and returned a kiss, as well. Everyone cheered the couple, except Two Hawks and Clay Basket, who were both trying to get the two lovebirds' attention by clearing their throats to remind them that such public displays of affection were considered taboo among the people. It was clear to everyone that such attempts were futile. As the two continued to kiss and embrace, the people continued to cheer, and Gideon howled in approval.

28

It was March of 1822. Azariah Hancock, his pregnant wife, Sweet Grass, their dog, Gideon, and Liam O'Reilly had just returned to the Arapahoe village of White Antelope in the Wind River Mountains two weeks prior. Outside the lodge of his in-laws, the now sixteen-year-old mountain man known as He Who Walks Tall was pacing back and forth and sweating like a pig, while his beloved wife was in labor.

"Will you stop doing that!" shouted Liam. "Jesus, Mary's mother, and Joseph, you're the one that is about to become a father, but you're making me nervous!"

"I am just scared, that's all," said Azariah.

Two Hawks, Howling Wolf, Wandering Bear, and Night Wing just chuckled at him. They were there for support, while their women were with Sweet Grass inside, helping her bring in the new life.

"In all my years," said Wandering Bear, "I have never seen a man as nervous about fatherhood as you are, He Who Walks Tall."

"Can you blame him?" said Two Hawks. "The first time is always the scariest."

"Having the baby is not what worries me," said Azariah in the Arapahoe tongue. "I want everything to be all right. I want Sweet Grass and the baby to both be healthy and well when it is said and done."

"Have faith, my brother," said Howling Wolf. "My sister and the baby that is coming will be fine."

"You can't tell this fool to have faith," chuckled Liam. "Ever since Sweet Grass got pregnant, he has been trying to do all the housework himself, while she just lies down and rests for the entire pregnancy!"

"You jest," said Two Hawks.

Liam shook his head and laughed. "Getting a woman to lie down for nine moons while the man does all the chores would drive her to insanity!"

All the men laughed at Azariah's expense. At the same time, they gave him encouragement and comfort as he continued to pace. "Be calm, He Who Walks Tall," said Wandering Bear. "Women have been having babies since time immemorial."

"I know, I know," said Azariah. "But it still makes me nervous!"

Azariah had every reason to be nervous. While pregnancy and childbirth were always considered a joyous blessing, it was also very dangerous. Death from childbirth was not uncommon. Liam O'Reilly joked that he couldn't count the number of times he found the father-to-be on his knees, praying that Sweet Grass would come through and deliver a healthy baby. Jokes aside, however, the Irishman, as well as many of their Arapahoe friends, strongly sympathized with Azariah, and they too prayed for successful delivery. It was at that exact moment that the sound of a baby was heard wailing from inside the lodge. Azariah and all the men present stood in anticipation; Gideon was on all four paws, wagging his tail as if he knew the outcome. The deerskin hide flap opened and Black Shawl appeared with a huge smile on her face.

"You have a beautiful and healthy son, He Who Walks Tall."

Azariah collapsed to his knees with a huge sigh of relief, while

Liam, Two Hawks, and everyone present yipped, whooped, and cheered to high heaven. Gideon joined in the celebration with a couple of barks, wagging his tail and giving his master a saliva bath all over his face as if to say congratulations!

Before getting back on his feet, the new father asked Black Shawl if Sweet Grass was all right.

Black Shawl nodded and smiled at him as she held the flap open for him. "She waits for you," she said. "Along with your new son."

Inside the lodge, the new mother held her tiny infant, who had stopped crying and was sucking on his fingers. Azariah slowly approached his wife and new son. Tears of joy were falling down both sides of his cheeks as he got a good look at the infant.

"Do you wish to hold your son, husband?" asked Sweet Grass. Azariah nodded and gently held out his huge hands as Sweet Grass gave the baby to him. The boy looked like a full-blooded Arapahoe, with the exception that his eyes were blue, and he had his father's forehead and big nose. Azariah smiled as he cradled his new pride and joy in his arms, gently touching the baby's tiny hands with a forefinger.

"What shall we name him?" asked Sweet Grass.

"His last name is Hancock," said Azariah. "I have always liked Adam, Adam Hancock."

"It is a good name," said Howling Wolf as he entered the lodge followed by his father, Liam, Wandering Bear and Night Wing and Black Shawl.

"He must have an Arapahoe name as well," said Azariah. "For he is both white and Arapahoe."

"Agreed," said Two Hawks.

"Any candidates?" asked Liam. "You have any ideas, my love?" asked Azariah to Sweet Grass.

Sweet Grass was in thought for a moment and then noticed the baby playing with his father's bear claw necklace, from his first grizzly bear kill. "How about Bear Claw?"

Azariah thought for a moment and then his face lit up in approval. "Adam Bear Claw Hancock," he said. "I love it!"

"So do we," said Two Hawks with his arm around Clay Basket. "Well done, my daughter!"

With his new son still in his arms, Azariah approached his mother and father-in-law and gently handed them their new grandson. Clay Basket gently held the baby in her arms, while she and his grandfather beamed with pride. Wandering Bear started to chant and sing in the Arapahoe tongue, thanking The Man Above for this beautiful blessing that has been bestowed upon the family. Liam himself silently said a prayer of thanks to the Creator, and Azariah, holding Sweet Grass' hand, shouted a prayer of thanks to Jesus Christ for the birth of his new son and that Sweet Grass was well.

Later that evening, Sweet Grass had just finished feeding Adam Bear Claw and gently put him in his new cradle that his father had made two days ago. As she sang in her native tongue to rock her tiny infant to sleep, Azariah gently stood over both of them and placed his arm over her shoulder as he beamed with pride, while looking down at his brand new son. "He is beautiful," he said. "Like his mother."

Sweet Grass turned and smiled up at her husband and gently laid her head on his chest. "Do you miss your family?" The question caught Azariah a little bit off guard, but then he pondered for a moment.

"I do," he said. "I often wonder about Abigail and my parents; if they are still alive and if she is married."

"You have rarely spoken about them," said Sweet Grass. "But I know you think of them often."

"I do," said Azariah. "But it is not for me to know about their situation." Sweet Grass was a little surprised by her husband's statement. "God in His own good time will reunite me with my folks," said Azariah. "That is if it is His will. Otherwise, my place is here by your side, for as long as you will have me."

"Then you shall be by my side forever," said Sweet Grass. "Until our last breath."

zariah smiled and gently kissed his wife then suddenly picked
p and carried her to their sleeping place. "I will never leave your
e," he said. "For we are one on this path as God has chosen for us."

EPILOGUE

Back in Montgomery County, Maryland at the Hancock residence, Reverend Nehemiah Hancock sat on his front porch in his rocking chair, with a small child on his lap. The boy appeared to be one, going on two years of age. Humming one of his favorite gospel hymns, the forty-four-year-old giant gently tickled the little boy, making him laugh in delight. The past two years had been far from easy for the reverend, his wife, Abigail, and their only daughter, Little Abigail.

Not long after Azariah avenged her brutal rape and had to make his forced departure from their home, exactly two years ago, she found out that she was pregnant with the young toddler, who now sat on her father's lap. There was no question who the father was, and even though it was not her fault, Abigail wasn't sure if she could give the baby up for adoption or secretly abort it. Unlike most women in her situation, though, Abigail's parents were strongly supportive of her. Nehemiah discouraged his daughter from having an abortion but did tell her if she decided to keep the baby or give it up for adoption, he and her mother would always support her one hundred percent. It was a tough decision for the fourteen-year-old rape victim, now mother-to-be. Her parents' support, comfort, and encouragement hings a lot easier. The family even got surprise support from friends, the Allen family. Young Jason Allen in particular ged that he would be there for Abigail and the child, if she chose eep it, in the best way he possibly could.

The decision wasn't easy, but she told her parents that she was eeping the baby. On December 1, 1820, she gave birth to a healthy baby boy, whom she named Caleb Nehemiah Hancock. The only people who knew the child's paternity were the reverend, his wife, and the Allen family. Since the attack, Little Abigail, as she was still called by her father, never went to town, for she didn't want Sheriff Frederick Jones to know that he had a grandson, not that he probably cared anyway. Jason Allen, with the reverend's permission, would escort Little Abigail and her mother to town and back, while armed. The good reverend would babysit his grandson and sometimes take him over to the Allen plantation and spend time with them. On days such as this, he would sit in his rocking chair, with his grandson in his arms or on his lap as he got bigger and ponder while staring west.

He was brought out of his reverie when a hand touched his shoulder. "Penny for your thoughts, Nehemiah," asked his wife. The good reverend just smiled at her, before returning his attention to Caleb, who by this time held his arms out to his grandmother.

"Gandma," he said.

Abigail gently took him from his grandfather and hugged him as the boy's mother approached from the kitchen in an apron covered with flour.

"Dinner will be ready soon," said Little Abigail. The little boy gently waved to her and got a gentle peck on the cheek from his mother in response.

"Boy is getting big," said Nehemiah.

"That is because he comes from strong stock," said Abigail. "From his mother's side."

Little Abigail smiled, but deep down she was still troubled. She loved her son deeply and never blamed him for how he was conceived. But it was clear that she saw a lot of Belshazzar Jones in

Caleb and that brought her much anguish. Sensing their dau melancholy, Nehemiah and Abigail invited her to stay awhii enjoy the scenery, before returning to the kitchen.

"You all right, child?" asked Nehemiah.

Little Abigail nodded. "It is beautiful today." As they looked in the forest of this terrific spring day, the family began to feel at peace "I wish Azariah was here," Little Abigail said suddenly.

"I miss him, too," added her mother. "I pray he is still alive."

Nehemiah finally stood and wrapped his huge arms around his wife, daughter and grandson.

"Wherever he is," he said, "at least he is safe and forever free."

Little Abigail looked up at her father with a quizzical look. "How do you know that, Papa?"

Nehemiah smiled and looked to the heavens, before returning his gaze to his daughter. "Because God is with him."

AFTERWORD

Author's Note:

I first became interested in the fur trade when I was stationed at Kadena Air Base in Okinawa, Japan during the summer of 2005. It was when I was watching the first episode of the TNT miniseries Into The West. This is when I first heard of the Christian mountain man Jedidiah Smith, who was played by Josh Brolin. Since then, I have read books, mostly biographies of famous mountain men like Smith, Jim Bridger, Joe Meek, Kit Carson, Tom Fitzpatrick, Edward Rose, Joseph Walker, Lancaster Lupton, William Bent, John Colter, Old Bill Williams, Zenas Leonard and Hugh Glass. I have also read historical novels around the fur trade by terrific authors like Win Blevins, David Robbins (who writes under the pseudonym David Thompson), John Killdeer, John Legg, Richard S. Wheeler, the late Terry C. Johnson, Lane R. Warenski, Terry Grosz, B.N. Rundell, Arley Dial, Porter Mills III, M. Wayne Zillman, and D.L. Bittick. Also, I have had the pleasure of viewing fur trade films like Across The Wide Missouri, starring Clark Gable, mountain men starring Charlton Heston, and the Academy Award-winning epic The

Revenant, starring Leonardo DiCaprio. However, I have als
interested in the culture plight of the American Indian since i
child, and I have also read books on different tribes such as the b
feet, Ute, and Cheyenne as well as read biographies on many An
ican Indian heroes like Sitting Bull, Gall, Geronimo, Quanah Park
and in modern times Dennis Banks, who is the co-founder of th
American Indian Movement.

Which brings me to the reason and purpose of this first book—this
series I have created. Writing this novel was a challenge because it
was very time-consuming, and procrastination and writer's block
were a challenge as well. As a history major and staunch pro-Amer-
ican Indian advocate, my goal was to tell a story about the fur trade,
but from an American Indian point of view, without the romanticism.
That in itself was a double challenge since the main protagonist is
white and I, as the author, am neither white nor American Indian.

I sought help and advice from two of my friends and classmates from
my alma mater at Montana State University in Bozeman, MT, who
are both American Indian. One is of Northern Arapahoe and
Yankton Lakota ancestry and the other is of Cheyenne, Crow, and
Cree ancestry. The information they have given me on many of the
different plains tribes that historically inhabited the northern Rockies
and Plains was both a strong and valuable addition to my own
research that I have done in making this first novel of my series.

Even though this is a work of fiction, I wanted to be as historically
accurate as possible, especially concerning the rivalry between
different tribes, the reason why many trappers fled civilization for the
wilderness, and slavery. Being a native of Maryland myself, I wanted
to tell the beginning of this story on the backdrop of slavery, and I
found that Montgomery County, Maryland, where I lived until
1989, was the largest slaveholding county in the state. Also, fourteen,
the age of Azariah, was historically accurate for those times in the

s. Most people back then either married young or started
king at a very young age, because people didn't live long back
n. This is why so many married couples you will find having from
s little as five to as many as thirty children. Also, it was not
uncommon for the husband to be in his late teens to early thirties,
while his bride is as young as eleven or twelve years old, because of
the high mortality rate. We also must remember, most marriages, both
white, black, and American Indian, even rich and poor, were not
based on love, but out of necessity.

Discussing the Blackfoot Confederacy and their dislike for the trappers or white men during this time is also accurate, depending on
who you ask. While I was a student at Montana State University, I
had the pleasure of visiting the Blackfoot Indian Reservation on
many occasions and talked with those who are familiar with the infamous Two Medicine River fight that took place in 1805 between
Merriweather Lewis and the young Piegan teenagers. I am not
passing judgment on anyone, but I do tend to side with the Blackfeet
on this issue since from what I heard, these boys were unarmed and
were just trying to make a name for themselves. You have to see it
from their point of view and culture. They didn't consider it stealing
horses, actual stealing, but capturing as a prize, and if you weren't
responsible enough to keep an eye on your horse, then it was your
fault, not theirs. Merriweather Lewis and his party had been out west
long enough to understand and know that many tribes practiced this
belief, so in my opinion, to shoot an unarmed teenager in the back for
attempting to steal your horse is inexcusable. I found out later information that another member of his party stabbed the other Piegan
teenager to death.

Before I end this note, I want to apologize to movie producer Jerry
Bruckheimer and actors Will Smith and Martin Lawrence for
borrowing a line from their blockbuster sequel Bad Boys 2. I believed
the line, "You look like you're at least thirty" would be a terrific

parody and even more hilarious being said in the 1820s and co from American Indians. I want to thank my friends, Candy Fe and Ryon Sun Rhodes for their help, advice, and their construct criticism in the making of this novel, and my parents, Lois and LeRo Peters, and my cousin, Nathan Peters Jr., for motivating me and pushing me to use my God-given talent in writing. To my sister, Lakeisha Peters Dickerson, for proofreading and editing my novel before I sent it to the publisher, and last but not least, I wish to thank my Lord and Savior Jesus Christ for giving me the gift to write and the mind to daydream stories that I wish to create.